"The house wasn't the way I'd left it," Will said.

"Things were moved around, kind of carelessly, too."

Caralee frowned, and he liked the way her mouth quirked up to one side in serious contemplation. It was nice to know she didn't instantly dismiss his concerns. He'd half thought she might.

"There was no one in there, not to my knowledge," she assured him. "But if you say things weren't as you left them—"

"They weren't."

"I'll look into it. Maybe the sheriff sent someone in and just forgot to tell me. I'll find out, Will, but you need to promise me you won't go back over there. Especially if someone has been tampering with the site. I need to know you aren't involved. Can you promise me?"

He met her eyes. They were such a deep blue, almost endless in color. They were earnestly searching his eyes, too. She wanted to trust him, he could see that. She just didn't believe she could.

He wanted more than anything to convince her.

Not the typical pastor's wife, **Susan Gee Heino** has been writing romance since the first day her dear husband bought her a computer, hoping she would help him with church bulletins. Instead, she started writing. A lifelong follower of Christ, Susan has two grown children and lives in rural Ohio. She spends her days herding cats and feeding chickens, crafting stories with hope, humor and happily-ever-afters. She invites you to sign up for her newsletter at SusanGH.com.

Books by Susan Gee Heino

Inspirational Cold Case Collection

Grave Secrets
Texas Betrayal

Visit the Author Profile page at LoveInspired.com.

BURIED THREAT

SUSAN GEE HEINO

LOVE INSPIRED
INSPIRATIONAL ROMANCE

LOVE INSPIRED®
INSPIRATIONAL ROMANCE

Recycling programs
for this product may
not exist in your area.

ISBN-13: 978-1-335-46839-0

Buried Threat

Love Inspired
22 Adelaide St. West, 41st Floor
Toronto, Ontario M5H 4E3, Canada
www.LoveInspired.com

Printed in U.S.A.

And [the Father] said unto him, Son,
thou art ever with me, and all that I have is thine.
It was meet that we should make merry,
and be glad: for this thy brother was dead,
and is alive again; and was lost, and is found.
—*Luke* 15:31–32

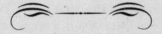

This book is dedicated to Cori Deyoe.
Your professionalism, dedication and insight
make you a wonderful agent and I'm so glad
you've worked with me all these years.
Your constant encouragement, kindness and humor
make you a wonderful human being
and I'm so glad you are also my friend.

I'd like to give a special thank-you to the
Richwood Police Department. I appreciate the time
your officer spent graciously answering my questions
about procedure and terminology, and I am grateful
for your vigilance here in our little village in Ohio.
Keep up the great work!

Chapter One

Caralee Patterson flicked her sunglasses out of her shirt pocket and quickly slid them on. The late springtime sun was bright after the past hour she'd spent in her grandfather's dim hospital room. It didn't help that her eyes stung from the tears she still fought to conceal. The last thing Grandpa would want was to see her crying over him.

The cancer had taken a toll, and now he was in the hospital with pneumonia. But he was slowly getting better and his desk was still waiting for him at the police station. He'd promised her he'd be back on the job soon, and she could only pray that would be true. He was the best police chief that Blossom Township had ever had, and Caralee felt woefully inadequate to be taking his place while he was out.

Grandpa had always been a larger-than-life figure. Growing up, Caralee had spent nearly as much time at his house as she had in her own. It was no secret how much she adored the big, bubbly guy. In fact, it was his influence that had led her to pursue a career in law enforcement. Following in his footsteps, she'd attended the academy and then gotten hired on here with the Blossom Township Police. Two months ago, Grandpa had had to take a leave of absence to start his cancer treatments. As the longest-serving member of their small local force, she'd become the youngest acting police chief in township history.

She had to admit that at twenty-seven years old, she didn't really feel qualified to take over his position— even if it was only temporary. Then again, it wasn't as if there was a lot of excitement here in Blossom Township. There were only six of them on the local police force, and none had been here longer than she had. Most of their officers saw Blossom Township as just a stepping stone to working in a more metropolitan area. Young people were hired right out of the academy, put in a couple years here, then went on to Cleveland or one of the larger forces nearby.

Caralee stayed because she couldn't imagine working anywhere else. She loved her quiet little town and didn't want to let anyone down. What if she couldn't handle things right as police chief? What if she made some mistakes? It would all be a lot easier when her grandfather was back on the job and things felt more normal again.

Her radio cracked on, the dispatcher calling for her attention. She quickly replied and let herself into her cruiser parked in the visitors' lot outside Blossom Memorial Hospital. She started the engine, put the windows down to get air moving and waited for dispatch to advise. Even with the breezes off Lake Erie, the sun was heating up now that it was early June.

"Officer DeKalb requests assistance," the dispatcher said.

"What's going on, Vicki?" Caralee asked, surprised she hadn't been told what sort of assistance was needed.

"He says he'll inform when you get there," Vicki said. "I'll send the address. You available?"

"Yeah, I just got done visiting Grandpa. He's feeling stronger and says hi to everyone."

"Glad to hear it. He's sure been in our prayers. We all miss him around here."

"So do I," Caralee said, putting the car in gear and backing out of the lot. "Anything I need to know before going on call?"

Vicki hesitated. "DeKalb will catch you up."

The computer lit up with the address. Caralee read it twice before recognizing it.

"He's at the old Viveners place?" she asked, just to be sure.

"Yeah. The quicker you can get there, the better."

She signed off, feeling an unexpected sense of concern. Violet Viveners had been dead for six years now, her house sitting vacant on Maple Street that whole time. It had become an eyesore, for sure, and Caralee hated to think what might've happened to motivate her young officer to call her out there.

Clearly it wasn't a dangerous situation—she would have certainly been notified of that. Most likely it was a case of vandalism. It was impossible for a house to sit empty this long without drawing attention from local kids with too much time on their hands. She sighed, wondering what had been done to the place this time.

Last year someone had expressed their artistic talents by spray-painting obscene images on the tall brick wall surrounding the backyard. The residents of Maple Street complained until the village council stepped in and paid to have the wall power-washed. Over the years, there had also been reports of things being thrown through the boarded windows, wild animals taking residence under the porch and attempted break-ins.

Worst of all, though, was the destruction to the landscaping. While Mrs. Viveners was living, she'd been renowned for her green thumb. The brilliant perennials, lush shrubs and waves of vivid annuals around her home always made Violet Viveners a local celebrity. Her daylilies especially were award-winning. The woman was a genius when it came to cultivating and creating beauty.

She had *not* been known for being friendly, however. With no living relatives and a husband who'd abandoned her years before, she'd seemed perfectly content to keep to herself. She doted on her gardens and was suspicious of visitors. While the front of the house was a showplace for the neighborhood, Mrs. Viveners's backyard oasis behind the high walls was hers alone—her own secret garden.

Only a select few Blossom Township residents had ever been invited to view the enclosure. Caralee had been one of them during her childhood—her mother had made friends with Mrs. Viveners, and the older woman had taken a special interest in young Caralee, who had been privileged to visit many times. They'd have tea in the garden, and Caralee would gawk in awe at the explosion of color and fragrance. Mrs. Viveners would walk with her, telling her in loving detail about each and every bloom. As Caralee got older, Mrs. Viveners had allowed her to help with weeding, watering and transplanting. Caralee had learned a lot from her afternoons in Mrs. Viveners's garden.

But that had been a long time ago. As Caralee had grown up, she'd spent less and less time in that secret garden. Mrs. Viveners had become more reclusive, then passed away six years ago. Caralee still felt a tinge of remorse any time she drove past the place and saw what it had become—dead, dreary, uncared for and unloved. She prepared herself for the worst as she approached the address.

As she pulled alongside the curb, the first thing she noticed was Officer DeKalb's cruiser parked out front. The second was the huge, rusted pickup truck parked in the driveway. And the next was a stack of lumber, freshly delivered, with miscellaneous power tools on the front porch and fresh panes of glass where the broken and boarded windows used to be.

Someone was working on Mrs. Viveners's old house! How long had this been going on? She hadn't heard of anyone buying it—hadn't even heard that the issues with the estate had been cleared up. Last she knew, the property was tangled up in legal matters since Mrs. Viveners had no heirs, and her estranged husband could not be located. Had that finally been resolved? Caralee quickly notified dispatch of her arrival and hurried up to the house in search of her officer.

DeKalb was waiting for her under the ornate brick archway between the garage and the house. The iron gate swung shut behind him as he came toward her. He seemed visibly relieved by her arrival.

"I'm glad you got here right away," he said, then his voice dropped as he glanced back over his shoulder. "I've been careful not to leave him alone back there."

Caralee frowned. "Who's back there?"

"The owner of the place, Willard Viveners."

Caralee caught her breath. She recognized that name—Mrs. Viveners had spoken of her missing husband more than once over the years. She hadn't had nice things to say about him.

"Willard Viveners is *here*?"

"Yeah, he's doing renovations. He says the old lady sure let everything go and he'll be lucky to get his money back out of it."

Caralee fumed. "He said that, did he?"

"He isn't really happy about having us here, actually, so…"

Caralee pushed past the officer and headed toward the imposing iron gate that protected the garden. If Mrs. Viveners's wandering husband was inside that garden, Caralee wanted to talk to him. What kind of man would leave his lonely, aging wife all alone like he had? Poor old Mrs. Viveners had struggled to keep up with everything on her own. How dare the old man complain about the condition of the place now!

DeKalb was saying something behind her, but Caralee was too busy with her own thoughts to hear him. What had happened to this house was a real shame. After Mrs. Viveners passed, several locals had wanted to buy it, to care for it and preserve the garden, but it couldn't be sold. The husband's name was on the deed, and it technically belonged to him. While he was off enjoying his golden years, his poor wife had died alone, and her beautiful garden was destroyed.

But he was back. Willard Viveners must be over seventy now, as his wife had been nearing it when she finally passed away. Why did he wait so long?

She would have kept right on marching into that backyard to find out, except that when she reached the iron gate, it swung open. She had to jump out of the way to avoid being smacked in the face. It caught her quite off guard.

So did the man who came striding through. This was *not* some elderly geezer. He wore a tight blue Penn State University T-shirt, jeans that seemed to have earned their ripped knees and work boots heavily caked in mud. His shaggy brown hair was uncombed, and he could use a shave.

This tall, broad-shouldered laborer who nearly flung the gate in her face couldn't have been more than two or three years older than she was. She eyed him, trying to reconcile his appearance with her expectations. He eyed her right back.

"You're not Willard Viveners," she said bluntly.

"I certainly am," he countered. "Who are you?"

At this point, DeKalb trotted up next to her to make a quick introduction. "Mr. Viveners, this is Chief Patterson."

The so-called Mr. Viveners looked doubtful. "*Chief* Patterson? No, you're not."

"I certainly am!" she replied, borrowing his own words. "Just what are you doing here on this property?"

"I own this property," the man said. "I'm renovating

it, or at least I *was*. Your officer here told me to stop. He said he needed to call his chief and…that's really you?"

"It is."

"Is there anyone on this police force who is legally of age?"

She bristled under his dubious gaze. "I assure you that Officer DeKalb and I are both old enough to do our respective jobs. Now, how about you just produce some kind of identification for us, *Mr. Viveners*, so we can get this situation sorted out."

"I don't think it's *my* ID you need to be worried about, Chief," the man said, holding the gate open as if to usher her inside. "It's the guy in the backyard you need to investigate."

Caralee didn't like the smug grin he gave her. She glanced over to Officer DeKalb. He looked admittedly pale.

"Who's in the backyard?" she asked him.

"That's why I called you out here, ma'am," the officer replied nervously. "I didn't want to put it over the radio until you were here to tell me how to proceed, but…"

"What's going on here, DeKalb?"

"Um, well… Mr. Viveners was working on clearing the brush and debris from the garden, and—"

The gruff man seemed to run out of patience. He interrupted the hesitant DeKalb to continue. "The place is a wreck. I was digging out some dead shrubs in the backyard, and…well, there's dead stuff I didn't plan for. It seems someone planted more than just daylilies out there."

She waited for him to continue. He was infuriatingly confident, staring back at her as if his cryptic words should've made perfect sense. They didn't. Angrily, she shrugged at him.

"And? Who am I supposed to investigate?"

"The corpse!" he said, rolling his eyes in frustration. "The person I just dug up in my backyard!"

She did *not* expect him to say that.

"You found a *body* in your backyard?" Hopefully her voice didn't betray the horrified shock she felt. "A *dead* one?"

"No question about that," the man assured her. "Whoever it is has been dead a long time, judging by the appearance of the remains and the size of those shrubs growing over that spot."

"What do we do now?" Officer DeKalb asked her.

Her first instinct was to run immediately to her grandfather and ask what he would do with something like this. People simply didn't find bodies buried in gardens here in Blossom Township. But no, she couldn't trouble Grandpa in his current condition. She had training for all sorts of scenarios; she could handle this.

"We'll do exactly what we're supposed to," she instructed her officer. "You'll continue to keep the scene secure, and I'll call the county sheriff's office. They've got a CSI unit."

"And what about me?" the unhappy workman grumbled. "I'm on a schedule here. I've got to get this place done so I can put it on the market."

"Your schedule went out the window the minute your backyard turned into a crime scene," Caralee informed him. "The only thing you'll be working on here is explaining to me how you can be Willard Viveners, when I know for a fact Willard Viveners is an elderly man."

Chapter Two

Will slapped the dirt off his jeans and watched the young police chief. She seemed awfully sure of herself, ready to argue with him when she clearly didn't have all the facts. Ordinarily he might enjoy sparring with her, an attractive woman who obviously could handle herself, but today he just didn't have the time. Every minute they wasted was money draining from his bank account.

"So you know Willard Viveners, do you?" he asked, not above giving her a cocky smile.

"No, but I knew Violet Viveners, and she told me her husband was even older than she was."

He considered her words and then nodded. "Yep, he probably was."

"So you admit you aren't him."

"I admit I wasn't married to Violet Viveners. That doesn't mean I'm not Willard Viveners."

Clearly this confused her, and she wrinkled her nose at him. "It doesn't tell me who you are, though."

"I told you who I am—Willard Viveners." He paused for dramatic effect, then added, *"Junior."*

He could see she was about to argue with him again, so he cut her off.

"The Willard Viveners who was married to Violet was my father. And no, I'm no relation to Violet, rest her soul. My mother lives in Pittsburgh."

To prove himself, he reached for his wallet. The young officer with her jumped to alert, his hand on his gun. *So much for small-town hospitality.*

"It's okay... I'm just getting my wallet."

"Keep your hands where we can see them," Chief Patterson ordered, but motioned for her officer to stand down.

She took the wallet suspiciously, flipped it open to his ID and eyed it for several moments. Finally, she sighed and handed it back.

"So you are who you say you are," she conceded. "Violet never told me her husband had a son."

"I doubt she knew about me." He shrugged. "From what the lawyer said when he contacted me about this place, my father wasn't exactly an upstanding family man. He left Violet, whispered sweet nothings to my mother, then left her before I was even able to walk. When they couldn't find him after Violet died, the estate finally declared him dead and started looking for his next of kin. It took the courts a while to track me down to tell me I'd inherited this house...and all the headaches that go with it."

If he'd been hoping for a heartfelt apology, he didn't get one. Chief Patterson was all business. "I'm sorry about the confusion, Mr. Viveners, but—"

"*Will.* Call me Will," he said, out of habit.

Being named after the heartless cheater who'd swept

his young mother off her feet and then abandoned her with a baby wasn't exactly something Will was proud of. Especially now that he could potentially add involvement in a murder to the list of his father's moral failings.

"All right, Will," she said. "I appreciate you clarifying things. Show me what you found."

The gate squeaked loudly as he led them into the backyard. There wasn't much of a yard out here, more like the remnants of pathways through patches of overgrown jungle. It was all such a mess that it was hard to imagine the place had ever been cared for at all. A lilac tree at the back corner still had a few fragrant blossoms, and little bits of color poked through here and there where something was trying to bloom. It all just seemed a useless mess to Will's eye.

"Here. I've been working along that far wall, but today I thought I'd tackle this thorny mess." He pointed to the area where he had managed a few shovelfuls before his discovery. "I started digging out this bush."

"The *roses*? You were digging up her *roses*?" Patterson asked. She sounded as if he'd been attacking the Mona Lisa.

He didn't bother to answer but might have possibly rolled his eyes. She leaned in to survey the earth. Her sharp gasp of breath and quick backward jump proved she'd seen what she came for.

"I stopped as soon as I uncovered it. Against my better judgment, I called you guys," he explained.

She nodded, her face showing a mixture of fascination and revulsion—much like he himself had felt. At first his brain hadn't wanted to comprehend what he saw. How could there be a human skeleton buried here

with the roses? He figured it was an old Halloween dec-
oration at first and even tugged at it a bit.

That was how he knew it was real. He'd discovered a
hand, the fragile bones long since deprived of their flesh
but still held in place by the very soil that had covered
them. Rotted fibers of the clothing that had once covered the rest of the body still clung in muddy folds over
it. Will had stopped before uncovering the head. That
excitement would be left for the professionals.

Patterson cleared her throat and composed herself.
"You got more than you expected with this inheritance,
huh?"

"So far I've gotten *nothing* with this inheritance,"
he snapped. "Except maybe nightmares for a lifetime.
I won't get anything out of this place until I can fix it
up and sell it. How about if you and Officer DeKalb
try to make sense of this horror, and I'll just go back to
work, okay?"

She shook her head. "Oh, no… I don't think that's
going to be possible. This house is a crime scene now.
Work will have to wait."

"I'll stay out of your way, don't worry. You'll be here
in the backyard, and I'll be inside the house. It's no
problem."

"It *is* a problem, Mr. Viveners," she insisted. "Until
we know what we're dealing with here, this whole property is off-limits for you."

"Off-limits? All of it? But it's my house!"

"And it's my crime scene. As of right now, I'm lock-
ing it down. Officer DeKalb can accompany you inside
to gather some things, then you'll have to leave."

"And go where? It's not like I've got a dozen other places to live, you know."

"Blossom Township has nice hotels and some bed-and-breakfast offerings," she stated, as if money was not even a consideration.

Maybe in her world it wasn't. In his, though, it was. Money for luxuries like hotels and cozy B and Bs was a bit beyond his budget. The last accommodations he'd had were…well, he hadn't exactly been a paying guest.

Officer DeKalb seemed a little more understanding. He cleared his throat before speaking. "Actually, ma'am, now that schools are letting out for the summer, those places are probably full with tourists already. And with the big Flower Festival coming up, you know they've been booked for a year."

This was no surprise to Will. The fact that a quiet village like Blossom Township even had a tourist season was the main reason he'd taken on the task of fixing up this old house in the first place. If he'd inherited this house anywhere else, he would've just hired an agent to sell it off for whatever they could get. When he'd done a little research into Blossom Township, however, he'd realized Violet Viveners's run-down old house could actually be a gold mine, if he was willing to put the effort into fixing it up.

Blossom Township was a picturesque lakeside village in northern Ohio, full of summertime charm and relaxation. All through the summer months, it was a busy tourist destination, with plenty of fishing and boating, and scenic parks, walking trails and sandy beaches to enjoy. There were concert venues and a popular summer theatre, rustic, covered bridges in the rolling hillsides and a quaint downtown area with art galleries, farm markets and boutique shops. In just the short time Will had been here, he'd watched the town fill up with families, retired couples and young people enjoying vacation away from whatever rat race they usually faced.

He could see the appeal, and he was more than eager to take advantage of it. His goal was to renovate the house as quickly and cheaply as possible, then sell it. That cash would be just what he needed to begin rebuilding some precious bridges he'd burned back home.

This body buried in his garden was not a part of his plan. He wasn't about to let a small-town cop put a halt to the progress he'd been making. It wasn't just a matter of greed—he *had* to get the work done and sell the place. Soon.

"So just where, exactly, do you expect me to go if I can't stay here, in my own home?" he asked sharply.

"There must be a vacancy somewhere," Chief Patterson said offhandedly. "I'm sure you'll find something."

"And what money am I supposed to use to pay for it?" he shot back. "I've sunk everything into this. I didn't really budget for a luxury vacation in some trendy B and B."

He hoped his admission made her uncomfortable. As much as he hated anyone knowing he was flat broke, he really hated being told what he could and could not do. It wasn't his fault someone had gotten themselves buried in the backyard. Why should he have to pay for it?

For a moment it looked like she was going to snap back with a snarky comment about it not being her problem, but she didn't. She paused and actually seemed to consider his words. When she finally responded, her voice was much less clipped and clinical.

"Okay, you're right. You can't stay here, but I'm not throwing you out on the street. I know someone who can help you."

He was almost afraid she'd recommend some half-way house out on the wrong side of the tracks, but she didn't. Her suggestion was far worse.

"I'll call my church," she said cheerfully. "Pastor Donaldson will be able to set you up somewhere."

He tried not to cringe. "I'm not looking for charity."

"Well, you can't stay here, Mr. Viveners."

"Will. My name is *Will*."

Her eyes narrowed and he noticed her hands clench, but she didn't give in to anger. Instead, she took a deep breath and turned to her officer.

"DeKalb, run out to my car, please. There's a small black binder on the passenger seat. Can you bring that to me?"

The young officer sprinted off toward her car. Will just glared at the police chief. To his surprise, she glared right back. She had striking eyes, a very dark blue that seemed impossibly serious—she was older than he'd first assumed. The freckles across her nose must have misled him, but there was no mistaking the confidence and commitment in her gaze now. Even as he took a step toward her, she didn't falter. Her gaze was steady, and she held her ground. He wondered if she'd still be quite so unflappable if she knew all about him.

"We will find you someplace to stay," she said firmly. "Pastor Donaldson has a lot of resources available to him. I'm sure he can—"

"I'm not staying with some preacher," he cut her off.

At last she was taken aback by his vehemence. "You…what? You have something against preachers?"

"Yeah. Let's just say I've had my fill, okay?"

"He's not going to preach at you, he's just going to help set you up somewhere until you can get back in your house."

"I don't care. I don't need him."

"You haven't even talked to him. He might be able to offer you—"

"I don't want what he's got to offer," he declared. "Compassion, concern, platitudes…whatever he's got, I've heard it all, and I see right through it. I'm not interested in anything your hypocritical reverend has for me."

"He's not a hypocrite," she retorted. Clearly, he'd struck a nerve. Her chin jutted and she snapped at him defensively. "I assure you, he's just a good man who can connect you with someplace to stay."

"With no strings attached, of course."

"Of course."

"I've heard that one before, too."

She didn't get a chance to continue the argument. The radio she wore clipped to her uniform crackled, and a voice called her name. She eyed Will but leaned in to respond to the radio.

The voice on the other end asked if she had anything to advise. She confirmed that she did—she needed another unit dispatched, and she said she'd been contacting the sheriff to assist. That didn't surprise Will; a police force in a town this size probably needed the extra manpower of the local sheriff for anything beyond the mundane.

And this was definitely not mundane. There probably had never been a body discovered in a garden here in Blossom Township. It would figure that the one time it happened, Will was involved. It seemed he was always in the wrong place at the wrong time.

Patterson finished her radio conversation. This investigation was off to a roaring start. No doubt there would be state representatives here, too. Will bristled at the thought of them all invading his home, displacing him whether he liked it or not.

He was already grumbling under his breath when Officer DeKalb came trotting back toward them. He handed the chief a black case. She unzipped it to reveal file pockets in a tidy binder. From one of those pockets she pulled out a business card, then from another she extracted a couple other cards. Gift cards? She held them out toward Will.

"Here. This is Pastor Donaldson's contact information. Call him, and Officer DeKalb can give you directions to the church if you want to go see him. These," she said, indicating the gift cards, "will help cover some of your extra expenses. There's a card for the gas station to cover any extra driving you might need to do, and you should be able to get some food on the others."

"I told you I don't want charity."

Her eyes flashed. "It's not charity, Mr. Viv—"

"*Will.* My name is *Will.*"

"Fine. It's not charity, *Will*, it's my job. I can't demand that you vacate your house if you don't have the means to do so. So call the church, let Pastor find you a place to stay and use the gift cards for whatever you need. I've got to talk to the sheriff and get him up to speed so he can advise his investigators." She nodded to her officer. "DeKalb, help him. See that he gets whatever he needs from inside, then escort him to his truck. This scene is officially off-limits to everyone but law enforcement. Make sure *no one* gets in."

Giving Will one last angry glance, she turned on her heel and headed out of the backyard. Will watched her go, torn between his dislike for her uniform and the strange, unexpected sense of admiration he was feeling. She might be the typical cocky cop who thought she had all the answers, but she wasn't afraid of him. He had to give her credit for that.

"Come on," Offer DeKalb prodded. "I'll follow you in so you can get your things."

"I don't have many things."

"Then it's not going to take very long, is it?" the young man said. "If you want, I can write down directions to the church."

"I won't be needing those."

"But you've got to find somewhere to—"

"I'm fine. I'll find somewhere."

The officer simply shrugged and ushered him through the door. Will pushed past him, heading inside. The place was a mess, tools and lumber scattered about, everything covered in drywall dust, but it was the only home he had right now. He wondered how long it would be until he was allowed to come back.

Hopefully, not too long. Because then it would be too late.

Chapter Three

It had been a long day. Caralee coordinated activities at the Viveners house while the county crime unit came out to begin the investigation. Today's focus had been on retrieving the remains and preserving the scene. Covering the whole yard, the garage and the interior of the house for any possible evidence would take a couple more days.

Caralee would oversee every aspect of the investigation, but the county CSI unit was at her disposal, and deputies would assist with securing the site. The body itself would go to the state crime lab for examination.

The rest of the day was filled with coordinating all these various agencies, and it was well after dark when the remains were finally fully sent on to the lab. Exhausted, Caralee found herself still filing reports in her office at midnight. Getting up from her chair before she fell asleep in it, she yawned and stretched her aching muscles. She would love to head home for bed, but this paperwork wasn't going to finish itself. Maybe another cup of coffee would help.

Before she could head for the break room, her radio crackled. The night dispatcher announced that a call had come in. Plopping back down in her chair, Caralee sighed. At this time of night, there was only one other officer on duty. And he was already busy with a theft report at the local car dealership. Dispatch wanted to know if Caralee could look into reports of an abandoned vehicle on the edge of town or if the call should be forwarded to the sheriff's office that handled their overflow.

An abandoned vehicle. It might very likely be related to the car dealership situation—no need to bring in the sheriff's office if the police were already handling it. Caralee drew a long breath and rubbed her aching forehead. It was a matter of pride when their little department could cover all their calls without resorting to help from the sheriff. Caralee clicked on her radio to reply.

"I'll respond. It could be a stolen vehicle from the call Sergeant Billings is on. Have him check in with me when he's free. Meanwhile, send me the location, and I'm on my way."

She shook off the tiredness and grabbed her things. Hopefully, this call wouldn't take too long—she'd just head out, run the vehicle's license or VIN and call for a tow. Maybe she could be back in the office in a half hour.

Driving the ten minutes across town gave her time to begin quietly processing some of the days' events. Would Grandpa be proud of how she'd handled it, or had she let things slip through the cracks? She'd done her best to give a strong, confident performance today, but that was all it was. Any confidence she showed was completely manufactured. She'd never had to take charge of something like a possible murder. And she'd certainly never encountered someone like Willard Viveners, Jr. She couldn't seem to get him out of her mind.

Where had he come from? Why had the small-town rumor mill not picked up on his arrival, or even the fact that he simply existed? Maybe she'd been too busy with work, or too concerned about Grandpa.

Or maybe Mr. Viveners—Will—had intentionally kept a low profile. What did she really know about him? Even with all the questioning and write-ups, she hadn't looked into the man's history. Out of curiosity—because for some reason she really was curious about him—she took advantage of a stoplight to quickly run his name through the Mobile Data Computer installed in her cruiser. What popped up was more than a little surprising.

There he was in a photo, with those unmistakable green eyes. He wore a stoic expression, and his hair was much more neatly cut than it was today. He was lacking the two-day-old scruff on his cheeks, too. But what stood out most about this photo was the word *Inmate* attached to it, the orange jumpsuit he wore and the bold identification number printed on a card.

Will Viveners was an ex-con! The light changed, but there was no traffic at this hour. Caralee kept her foot on the brake and quickly typed in a deeper search. What sort of person had she been dealing with today?

It was a relief to find that his record didn't indicate violence. He'd been convicted of fraud. Quite a lot of it, in fact. He and his business partner had duped a large number of vulnerable people with a real estate scheme. That caught her attention.

He had come to Blossom Township specifically to engage in a real estate transaction! So, even after serving four years in prison, he was right back in the very same line of work that had gotten him locked up. She couldn't believe this was a coincidence.

First thing tomorrow she was going to find Will Viveners. If he had plans to take advantage of anyone here, he'd better rethink them immediately. No faithless ex-convict was going to fleece anyone here, not under her watch.

But right now, she had a job to do. She was being dispatched to deal with an abandoned car, not dig up dirt on Will Viveners. There'd be plenty of time for that tomorrow. Closing the database, she hurried through the traffic light before it turned red again.

Her destination was just up ahead, so she radioed in to confirm her arrival. This part of town wasn't frequented by tourists. The buildings were run-down, and one of the streetlights overhead flickered, shining weak light at best. The address she'd been given was a vacant lot next to a paint supply store. She asked the dispatcher for confirmation on the type of vehicle she was looking for.

"The caller said it was an older model pickup truck. They weren't sure what make, just that it had been abandoned there."

Caralee could make out the vehicle parked at the back corner of a gravel lot, nestled up against weedy overgrowth. "I see it. Looks like a Chevy, definitely older."

"Want to read me the plates, and I'll run it for you?" the dispatcher asked.

"No need. I recognize it."

And she did. Her headlights fell on the old truck, and she knew it immediately. She'd seen it just a few hours ago parked in Violet Viveners's driveway. But why on earth had Will abandoned it here? This over-grown parking lot wasn't anywhere near a hotel or another place he could have chosen to stay. Had something happened to him?

She pulled into the deserted lot. Obviously, this old truck hadn't been here very long. Why would someone have called about it already? Something seemed off.

Considering what she'd just found out about Will Viveners, she decided to use extra caution. She parked the cruiser with lights still shining on the truck and grabbed her flashlight. Approaching slowly, she raked the light over the area nearby. There was no sign of anything unusual, just bits of old trash caught up in the weeds.

She came in closer, not sure what she was expecting to find. Foul play of some sort? The truck seemed deserted, the windows partially lowered. Shining her flashlight into the cab of the truck, she approached with caution.

Suddenly, Will suddenly popped into view. Caralee jumped. Apparently, he'd been sleeping there in his truck!

"What on earth…?" he yelled out.

She took a step back. "Mr. Viveners. What are you doing out here?"

He blinked in the bright light and angrily opened the door. "I was trying to sleep. What are *you* doing out here, shining that thing in my face and giving me a heart attack?"

"We had a report of an abandoned vehicle."

"As you can see, it is *not* abandoned."

"I see that."

"So you can just turn off that solar flare and head back to your police station."

"And you're just going to stay here? In your truck? In this parking lot?"

"Yes, unless you've decided I can go back to my house."

"It's a sealed crime scene," she reminded him, although she doubted he'd forgotten.

"Then I guess I'm staying here."

"But you can't."

"I assure you, I can," he stated. "And what are you doing out here in the middle of the night?"

"I'm on duty. Now, come on. Start it up, and I'll follow you over to the hotel."

"I'm not staying there."

"Look, you can't just sleep in your truck. This is private property, and you're trespassing. If you truly can't afford it, I told you Pastor Donaldson can help out. He's got a real heart for—"

"I don't need help from your preacher!" he said sharply, then immediately took a deep breath and lowered his voice. "Sorry, it's just… I'm not staying at a hotel—I already checked. You've got two hotels in this town, and they're both full."

"I see. Well, then, I'll just take you to the church."

He grumbled under his breath and climbed out of his truck. She took another step back. Adrenaline kicked in to wipe out all traces of the tiredness she'd felt; training kicked in to remind her how to handle a tense situation.

"There's no need to get out of the truck, Mr. Viveners," she said slowly, calmly. "We can resolve this. Just tell me how I can help. If you won't go to the church, maybe I can call Pastor for you."

Before he could answer, another bright beam of light shone on them both. Caralee turned to find a second police cruiser pulling into the parking lot, the side spotlight aimed their way. Ah yes, she'd asked to have Sergeant Billings check in with her in case this so-called abandoned vehicle was connected to the occurrence at the car dealership. Instead of calling or radioing, he must have simply come straight over.

Judging by the nervous way Will's gaze shifted now, and the white-knuckle grip he had on the door of his truck, Caralee wasn't so sure Billings's arrival was a good thing. She had the feeling Viveners was a man who was just a bit closer to the edge than she had first thought. His resentment at any mention of the church, coupled with his willingness to sleep in his truck rather than accept assistance, indicated a man with some baggage.

The arrest record and prison term she'd found kept racing through her mind. It would be foolish to ignore them. Will Viveners was a criminal. He'd spent four years locked up in close quarters with other criminals. Whatever he'd done to get him to that point and whatever he'd experienced afterward would have certainly affected how he thought, how he reacted to things. He was already upset with her. She really didn't know what he might do when confronted by two officers giving him orders.

"This guy making trouble for you, Caralee?" Billings called from his car.

She tried not to cringe in frustration. The last thing she needed was the sergeant undermining her authority by using her first name and implying that she couldn't handle whatever situation she was in.

"Everything's fine here, Sergeant," she barked back.

"Everything's fine?" Will repeated with a dubious sneer. "So we're good, are we? You and your sergeant will say good-night and just leave me in peace?"

"We're going to help you find someplace comfortable and safe for the night," she said diplomatically.

Will snorted, as if he didn't believe for one minute that she could do that.

Billings must have heard the snort all the way from his car. He came flying out, storming toward them. He shined his flashlight in Will's eyes and held his hand uncomfortably close to his weapon.

"You being difficult, bud?" he inquired, bearing down on Will. "What brings you all the way out here at this time of night, anyway? Doing some partying?"

Caralee wished she could simply shush her sergeant, but that would give the impression he wasn't an officer of the law to be taken seriously. The more he scanned Will and his truck with obvious disdain and suspicion, though, the more Will was going to lose respect for both of them and ruin Caralee's attempts to get him to cooperate.

"I was trying to sleep," Will grumbled, then turned on Caralee. "You felt like you needed to call for this guy to come back you up?"

"Does she need backup?" Billings questioned. "You planning to give her a hard time?"

"I was planning to be left alone!" Will griped.

"He was just sleeping here," Caralee said, giving her sergeant a warning glare and hoping he would take the hint to give up the posturing. "Turns out this has nothing to do with the theft at the car dealership you were working on."

"That's for sure." The sergeant chuckled. "No one in their right mind would steal this junker. You want to show me your registration?"

"You want to tell me why I need to?"

She put herself between them. "All right, stop. There's no reason for this. Sergeant, everything is under control. Mr. Viveners has been displaced and was just looking for a quiet spot to sleep tonight. I was explaining that there are better options than this parking lot."

"And I was still waiting to hear those better options," Will said. "But all I keep hearing about is your wonderful church."

"It *is* wonderful, and I know we can find a solution here," she said with a practiced tone, then turned to speak quietly to Billings. "Let's de-escalate this, Sergeant. He's had a rough day."

"Maybe he's trying to drown his sorrows, then. Have you performed a sobriety test?"

"I'm not a drunk!" Will growled at them. "And if you're going to stand right there and talk about me, you might as well come over here and say it to my face."

"You've got a bad attitude," Billings said.

Caralee could see anger boiling in Will's eyes. She moved toward him, but Billings did the same, and he stepped squarely on Caralee's foot. She gritted her teeth at the pain and and tried to move out of the way, but all that did was put Sergeant Billings off-balance.

He lurched forward. Will reacted instantly and put his hands up to defend himself.

Caralee could have guessed what would happen next, but there was nothing she could do about it. The sergeant saw Will's move as offensive. He grabbed Will, trying to turn him around and pin his arm behind him. Will resisted, probably on instinct.

"Back off!" he shouted.

Billings did not. He just applied more force to maneuver Will into a submissive posture. "Get down on the ground. Get down now!"

Will struggled, pulling his arm away from the sergeant. Caralee worried what he might do with that arm. The anger she'd seen on his face was quickly turning to rage, perhaps even desperation. Things were about to get ugly.

"Will, stop. Just stop," she said as calmly and firmly as she could.

Her words somehow got through. Will's eyes met her own; he glared but complied. He stopped resisting and dropped down to one knee. However, Billings hadn't been expecting this. He was still putting pressure on Will. When Will shifted position, Billings didn't adjust. He stumbled over Will's leg, clocking Will in the face with his elbow on the way down.

Will whirled on the sergeant, his fist flying to defend himself. Billings was too close; Will's fist landed square on his jaw. Billings swore loudly, then landed back in the gravel.

"That's it, buddy," Billings snarled, crawling back up to his feet and glaring daggers at Will. "You're going down."

Caralee put herself between the two men. "That's enough, Sergeant. He's done. You're done. This is over."

"Yeah, it is," Billings said, rubbing his jaw. "That's assaulting an officer. We all know what happens next."

Caralee sighed as Billings pulled out his handcuffs. This wasn't the solution Caralee wanted, but it seemed she'd finally found the place for Will Viveners to spend the night. He must have figured it out, too, because he looked right at her. All his swagger and cocky defiance was gone.

"No. Please don't," he begged.

She didn't want to. There was nothing else she could do, though. He'd just punched a cop. She sighed and gave Billings his orders.

"Take him into jail, Sergeant."

"My pleasure," Billings said, grabbing Will roughly.

Will remained passive and offered his wrists for the cuffs. Caralee met his eyes. Instead of anger or insolence, all she saw now was pain. And the deepest, coldest loss she'd ever seen on a man's face.

Chapter Four

Caralee adjusted her precautionary mask as she left the elevator to head toward her grandfather's hospital room. She hadn't slept much last night and hoped he wouldn't be able to tell how troubled she actually was by everything that was going on. He needed to focus on recovery, not worry about police work.

"He just finished his breakfast," one of the nurses at the desk said when Caralee greeted her. "His appetite is definitely getting better, so that's a great sign."

"Glad to hear it," Caralee replied. *All the more reason not to trouble him with work matters.*

She knocked lightly on Grandpa's door. He called for her to enter. The room was bright, the curtains thrown back with two lush bouquets basking on the windowsill. He was propped up in his bed and grinned when he saw her.

"So you haven't had enough of this place?" he joked. "You keep coming back."

"And I will continue to until you finally get booted

out of here," she assured him. "I hear you had a good breakfast."

"As good as a hospital poached egg can be," he said with a shrug. "The sausage was nice and bland, though. So how are things out in the world today?"

"Oh, just the usual," she said as casually as possible.

"Yeah? Just the usual bodies turning up in back-yards?"

"How did you hear about that?!"

He laughed at her. It was good to hear him laugh. "I may be stuck here out of commission, but I've still got connections."

"It was Sheriff Lee, wasn't it? He told you they'd sent in the CSI unit."

He must have noted the annoyance in her voice. She should've hidden it better.

"Now, now…don't be sore. It's not that he doesn't think you can handle it."

"But it's that he thinks you'd handle it better," she finished for him.

"He wanted to hear my ideas on the situation. Barry Lee and I have worked together a long time. He's my friend, Carebear."

She cringed at the childhood nickname he still used for her. Just another reminder that she would never truly be able to fill his shoes. "I wish he'd come to me if he's got questions."

"And I'm sure he will. So, since you were clearly not going to tell me about this, why don't you go ahead and fill me in now that I already know?"

"What's to fill in? I'm sure Sheriff Lee told you ev-erything."

"Well, he didn't know much about the fellow who found the body. The new owner of the place…what's his name?"

"Will Viveners, if you can believe it. He's the long-lost secret son of the old Willard Viveners. Apparently, the lawyers finally found him, and now he's inherited the place. He's trying to fix it up and sell it quick. I don't know, but…"

"But what?"

She hesitated to burden him with more of her troubles, but at this point she might as well. He was obviously interested and wasn't likely to drop the subject now that Sheriff Lee had spilled the beans.

She filled her grandfather in on the situation, explaining that the investigation had left Will Viveners temporarily homeless. She also told him about Will's conviction and prison time, and about her concerns regarding real estate fraud. Grandpa just nodded as he listened. He seemed far less worried about Will than she would have expected.

"So he's an ex-con trying to get his life back on track," Grandpa said. "He did the right thing when he found the body even though he must have known it would interrupt his plans, and that's not so bad. What's he doing now while you've got his house off-limits to him?"

"Well…that's the big problem, Grandpa. Right now he's cooling his heels in my lockup."

"He's in our jail? What on earth for!"

"He sort of punched Sergeant Billings last night."

"So he *is* a violent man."

"No, Billings started it—you know how he is. Will was upset with me for putting him out of his house, then

Billings stepped in because he didn't think I could handle it. He slammed Will with his elbow, so Will reacted. I don't know what to do, Grandpa. Billings has a bad attitude and I should have dealt with it before now. It's my fault things got out of hand and now there's a guy in my jail who really shouldn't be there."

Grandpa sighed. He knew Billings the same as she did; ever since the sergeant came to Blossom Township he'd had something to prove. Caralee had put off speaking to him about his attitude because, frankly, she wasn't sure he would listen to her. Now she regretted her hesitation.

"So you put this Viveners in jail for resisting arrest?" Grandpa asked.

"No, I just charged him for vagrancy. To be honest, I'm kind of surprised he didn't want to file charges against Billings. That's all I need right now."

Grandpa's smile was full of reassurance. "But now you've got an innocent man in jail, and Billings thinks he's innocent, too."

"Yeah."

"Are you sworn to serve Sergeant Billings, or the people of this community, Caralee?"

"The people, of course, which is why I can't just let Will Viveners go free. He *was* vagrant last night, and he *did* scuffle with Billings. What will people say if I just ignore what happened?"

"Clearly, you can't just ignore it. Billings needs a good talking to, and that Viveners fellow needs to stay someplace other than jail."

"I know. But where else can he go? He's broke, the

hotels are all full, and he won't consider charity. I can't let him go back to trespassing somewhere."

"He's not after handouts? That's honorable."

"He's stubborn and opinionated."

"Or maybe he's independent and principled. Why don't you find him some work? Get him someplace to stay where he's working for his keep."

"Grandpa, I'm not an employment agency! How am I supposed to find him something like that?"

"Surely there's somebody with an empty house who would love a temporary caretaker for it. Somebody laid up in the hospital, for instance, wondering how his grass is going to get cut and the plants are going to get watered. Somebody with a granddaughter who could check in on the guy every couple days and make sure he's doing okay."

She could hardly believe what she was hearing. Was he honestly suggesting Will Viveners stay at his house? An ex-con? Grandpa always did have a heart for mission work, but this was going too far.

"Oh no, don't even think about it, Grandpa! You don't know this guy—you can't invite him to live in your house."

"Why not? It's my house, after all, and it would help him out. It would help you out a bit, too, I think."

"But we don't know anything about him. You can't be serious about this, Grandpa."

"Things happen for a reason, Caralee. God brought him to our town, knowing the man would need a place to stay just when I happen to have an empty house. How can we not offer it?"

"But Grandpa...he won't want to stay at the police

chief's house. He wouldn't even let me call Reverend Donaldson. I think he's got some real issues with the church."

Grandpa just smiled. "All the more reason for us to show him Christlike compassion."

Just like that, Caralee knew she'd lost this argument. As usual, Grandpa was right. Will Viveners needed a place to stay, and the compassionate thing to do would be to let him use Grandpa's house. If he actually would be willing to pay for his keep by cutting the grass and looking after the place, it would be a real help to everyone. She sighed and reached out to take her grandfather's hand.

"All right. I'll invite him to stay at your place in exchange for cutting grass and taking care of things. I'll give him a to-do list. Anything in particular you want me to add to it?"

"Well…there are some frozen casseroles that Mrs. Kirby made up for me to keep on hand. I sure could use help eating them. That young man might enjoy home-cooked meals if he's had such a rough time of it, don't you think?"

"You know, Grandpa, you are a pretty good guy," she said. "Fine, I'll offer Will your house and your food, but I just hope we don't regret it."

The older man simply sighed and leaned back in his hospital bed. Caralee could tell he was getting tired. This pneumonia on top of his cancer treatments was certainly taking a toll on him. Despite it all, though, his smile of contentment was just as bright as ever.

"Never get weary of doing good, Caralee. When God

gives us the opportunity to share His love with some-one, there's no regret."

"If you say so, Grandpa. Still, I'm going to solve this case as fast as I can to get Will Viveners back into his own house and out of our hair."

"No, I'm not taking your charity!" Will grumbled.

He'd been uneasy and agitated ever since this so-called police chief had locked him up in here last night. Now she thought he'd leap for joy when she appeared with her self-righteous offering this morning? A sleep-less night in a small-town holding cell hadn't done much to improve his attitude. He was tired, grumpy and his face hurt where that hothead sergeant had slammed into him.

He supposed he should be grateful Chief Caralee hadn't made a bigger case against him—her bullying sergeant certainly had wanted her to. But she'd been fair. She might be annoying and nosy, but she seemed like a decent cop. She'd lectured Billings on de-esca-lation and locked Will up for misdemeanor vagrancy. The fine for that, apparently, was admitting to being a charity case.

"It's not charity," she insisted, crossing her arms in frustration as she glared at him through the cell bars. "I told you, the owner of the house would expect you to earn your keep while you're there."

"So it's forced labor, is it?"

"It's a mutually beneficial transaction. Look, I'm not holding you here. You're free to go, but if I find you trespassing in someone's parking lot again, you'll have to spend another night in here. I might not be so understanding for a second infraction. Since you can't get a hotel and won't accept charity, I thought this might be a good option for you. You'd cut the grass, bring in the newspaper…the owner even wants you to help eat the food in the freezer. If that's too much forced labor for you, though…"

"Why would this benevolent homeowner trust me in their house? What's in it for them?"

"What's in it for him is the comfort of knowing someone is looking after his house while he's laid up in the hospital. It's been a real worry, and he feels bad asking people for help. I guess you can understand that feeling, huh? It would help him a lot—and take the pressure off everyone else—if you'd just agree to this and be grateful."

"So who is he?"

She paused before she answered. He knew that probably meant something.

"He's my grandfather."

If her expression hadn't been so serious, he'd have thought she was joking.

"Your grandfather?"

"Yes."

"So…you're okay with letting me out of jail to go stay in your grandfather's house?"

"Should I not be okay with it?"

"Well, it's not like you really know me."

"I know *about* you," she said, her voice just chilly enough to assure him she did. "I know this isn't the first time you've been locked up."

Of course she would have seen his record, read all about his so-called crimes and the time he'd served in prison. He wasn't surprised at all she knew about that. He was, however, floored she would still invite him to stay at her grandfather's.

"You're sure he's okay with having me stay there?"

"He's got a soft spot for people in trouble. He's also the chief of police here."

"I thought *you* were the police chief."

"*Acting* police chief. Once he's recovered, he'll be back in his old job here. I hope."

"So, what will you be doing when you're not acting police chief anymore?"

"I'll still be a cop. So come on, are you going to help him out and go stay at his place, or are you going to be a pain in the neck and get yourself locked up again for sleeping in a parking lot?"

He had to laugh at her. "You're not offering this out of the kindness of your heart, but just because you don't want to deal with me."

"I told you this wasn't charity. You'll be helping him out because you'll be working for him, and you'll be helping me out by staying out of my hair while I've got a murder investigation going on."

"You're sure it's murder?"

She shrugged, careful to avoid discussion of an ongoing case. "I'm proceeding with that assumption until someone tells me otherwise."

"If they can tell us anything after all this time," he said. "Who knows how long he's been out there? Decades, maybe."

"All the more reason to keep you out of the way while we do our work."

"Seems like you'll have your work cut out for you."

"So will you, Viveners," she said. "Now come on. Your truck's still in impound, so I'll give you a ride over to my grandpa's house."

"But I'll need my truck!"

"It's Saturday. Impound won't open until Monday. You'll get it then."

"I have to wait two more days? What am I supposed to do for transportation?"

"You won't need it. Grandpa's got plenty of food there and a nice long to-do list for you. You won't need to go anywhere."

"But I…can I at least stop over at my place? I need to check on something."

"Your house is a secure crime scene. I've got guys looking after it. It's fine."

"But I…okay, whatever. How far away does your grandfather live?"

"The other side of town. Not far at all. And I'll expect you to stay there so I can keep an eye on you. Got it?"

He tried not to be angry. This whole thing could have been a lot worse—he could've been charged with resisting arrest or even assault. Acting Police Chief Patterson was at least being fair with him, not covering for Billings's actions or making Will take the blame for them. Some other police chief might've been hauling him into court right now. He supposed he should be thankful. But things didn't usually work out so well for him, so he wasn't entirely sure he could trust this.

"Fine," he said, stepping back from the door as Caralee unlocked it. "I'll go quietly, Chief."

Chapter Five

Caralee parked her cruiser under the shade of the old sycamore tree she must have climbed a hundred times as a girl. Grandpa's house sat in front of her, looking lost and forlorn without his reassuring presence in it. What was she doing, bringing this convicted criminal to stay here?

"Nice place," Will said from the seat beside her.

"It's been in the family for a while," she said. "Get your stuff and come on."

"My *stuff* is still in impound," he grumbled, but grabbed the bag he'd been given with the few personal things he'd had on him when she took him in.

"Monday," she reminded him, slamming her car door and crunching up the gravel walkway toward the front door.

Her grandfather's father had built this house many years ago. Three generations of Pattersons had spent lifetimes here. She really hoped they wouldn't end up regretting Grandpa's generous actions. Could they actually trust Will Viveners to take care of the place? He seemed to be surveying it with a keen eye, she noted. His gaze followed the lines of the roof as if he was counting the windows and doors. Probably memorizing the points of entry, casing the joint.

Then again, he wouldn't have to break into the place; they were giving him the keys. If he had any nefarious plans for the place and Grandpa's things in it, they were making it very easy for him.

"Mid-century Colonial Revival style," he said, assessing the house with scholarly precision. "Sits on a pretty big lot, nice shed in the back."

"Um, yeah. My great-grandfather bought three lots here and put this house right in the middle."

"Was he the police chief, too?"

"Nope, welder. Come on, I'll show you where you'll be staying."

She led him up onto the front porch and selected Grandpa's key on her keychain. It gave her a moment of hesitation when she realized she would probably have to give it to Will. Grandpa was so sure he wanted to help this guy, but she wished she felt more confident this was the right thing to do. Biting her lip, she opened the door and led Will inside.

"You can leave your shoes here, on the mat," she instructed. "My grandma never liked shoes in the house."

"A neat freak, huh?"

"A little bit. She's been gone almost four years now, but we all try to keep the place up to her standards. There's no food here in the front room. Kitchen's back through there, and beyond that is the den. That's where the TV is. Grandpa's room is in back, but it's off-limits. You'll be staying upstairs."

She started up the stairway. He followed, then paused on the landing. She glanced back to see what held him up. He was studying the series of family pictures hanging on the wall.

"Is this you as a kid?" he asked, grinning up at her.

She rolled her eyes. "Yes, that's me and my brother down at the creek."

"I'm surprised your neat-freak grandma put this photo on her pristine wall. Is that mud or slime smeared all over your face?"

"Algae," she corrected. "My brother thought it would be hilarious to throw it at me. But you'll note that he's covered in a lot more of it than I was."

"I see that. Looks like you could hold your own."

"I still can, don't ever doubt that," she warned. "And so can my grandpa, so look after his things carefully while you're here, got it?"

"Got it."

He followed her the rest of the way up, and she showed him the bathroom and guest room he'd be using. The room had been her father's, once upon a time. Now it was set up with two twin beds for when the grandkids visited—back when they still were grandkids. Her generation was all grown up now, with her youngest cousin just heading for college. It was doubtful the room had been used at all in recent years.

Will scanned it with a critical eye, taking in the blue gingham curtains, the handmade quilts on the beds, the vintage styling of the old desk in the corner. What was he thinking? Did he realize all the happy memories that lingered here? All the well-used board games, toy dinosaurs and stuffed animals that were still boxed up in the closet? Or did he just think the place needed some upgrades before it could be sold for a profit?

Convicted of real estate fraud. Her mind just would not let her forget it, and she didn't dare let her guard down. Yes, it was a good thing to help the man—and she loved Grandpa for his generous nature—but she would be keeping an eye on Will. Maybe she could have gotten his truck out of impound for him today, but knowing he'd be stuck here this weekend gave her a little more peace of mind. Until the crime scene was clear and he could go back to his own home, she planned to watch him like a hawk.

"There sure are a lot of photos of you around here," he said, pointing to the framed collage hanging over the dresser.

"That's not *all* me," she said. "That's me, my brother, my cousins…"

"I always wondered what it would be like to have a big family."

"It's not too big. There are just seven of us."

"Well that's big compared to my family. I have no cousins that I know of."

"None? Didn't your parents have any siblings?"

He laughed, but it wasn't a happy sound. "No idea. You seem to know more about my father than I do, and my mother refuses to ever talk about her family. They weren't exactly supportive when I came along. A child with no father was an embarrassment. My mother was expected to choose—keep them or keep me. She chose me."

"Wow, I'm sorry to hear that."

He shrugged. "I never knew them, but she always

told me she made the right choice. And without my fa-ther around, it was just the two of us. I always wondered what it must be like to have photos like these around the house…other people who looked like me."

"It just feels…ordinary," she said, though it was hardly an adequate explanation.

How *did* it feel? She honestly had no idea how to put it in words. Family had always been such a huge part of her life, part of who she was. To imagine what it would be like to not have that…it was tragic. No wonder his life had taken such a difficult course. Where would hers have gone if not for all the nurture, support and faith her family had given her?

He stared at those photos on the wall, trying to make sense of a lifestyle that must feel completely foreign. How quiet his holidays must have been! How lonely. A lump started to form in her throat just to think of all he had missed out on over the years.

Well, she was not about to get emotional here. Best to quickly change the subject.

"Towels and linens are in the hall closet. Don't leave them lying around—there's a hamper by the shower. I think the first thing you should concentrate on today is the yard. Leave your stuff up here, and I'll take you down to the shed. You do know how to use a lawn mower, don't you?"

"A what?" he said with a snarky grin, then slipped into a cheesy old-time-gangster accent. "Before I got locked in the joint, ya see, we were cutting grass with scissors and using steam engines for trimmin' the hedge."

"Don't be funny," she said. "I just never bothered

to ask if you really can do all these things my grandpa needs."

"Well, I can. I think you'll find I'm pretty handy."

She hoped she could believe him. From what she could see of his work on the old Viveners house, he was competent enough, but what did she really know about it? It looked okay, but could she be sure he'd really done it right? What if instead of helping Grandpa, he made things *worse* around here?

He must've seen her doubts in her expression. She was trying not to show just how much she worried, but clearly she failed. She wasn't the only one, though. He was probably trying not to show how much her suspicions bothered him, but it was written all over his face.

"I won't mess it up," he said gruffly. "You asked me to do a job, and I'll do it well. For whatever reason, your grandfather trusts me. I appreciate that."

"Good. I'll be back later to check on your progress." She glanced at her watch, mostly because she was starting to feel a little too self-conscious meeting his eyes. "Right now I've got work."

"Well, that's something we've got in common, then, isn't it?" he said, dropping his little bag of possessions on the bench at the foot of the bed and wiping his hands on his jeans. "I've got some grass to cut, and you've got a forgotten murder to solve. Personally, I would much rather be mowing."

She refused to admit it, but the truth was, she completely agreed.

Will finished wiping the kitchen counter and double-checked the sink. All his lunch dishes had been washed and put away—the whole area was spick-and-span. He wondered if Grandma Patterson would have approved of his efforts. Surely Caralee would let him know if he had missed a spot or put something in the wrong place.

He glanced out the window and admired the work he'd done outside today. The grass was cut neatly, the edging trimmed. He'd worked until well after noon then come in for a much-needed shower. Lunch had been some frozen casserole he'd found in the freezer—a dish with chicken and rice that was surprisingly filling.

He would've much rather spent these past hours working on his own home, but there was satisfaction in knowing he'd been helping someone—even if it was Caralee's police chief grandfather. It had been a long time since Will felt he'd been of any use to anyone.

He dried his hands and checked the clock. Caralee had said she was coming to look in on him later. But he had a commitment to keep. He'd just have to risk missing Caralee's visit.

This house sat on a quiet street on the far west end of the little town. It was a nice area with larger lots and newer houses than where his place was located. Will could see the vast blue expanse of Lake Erie from the upstairs windows. All he could see from his own house were the walls of that garden and the backs of neighboring houses.

Will's house was about a mile away, a nice easy walk. He had asked Caralee to stop by there when they left the jail, but she'd refused. It was just as well. He needed to bring something with him.

He'd saved part of his lunch in a backpack and filled up a thermos of water. This would do nicely in a pinch.

Slipping them into the backpack and sliding his phone into his pocket, he let himself out the front door. He locked up behind him and put the house key in his pocket. It couldn't take too long to make the trip, could it? Maybe he'd even be back before Caralee knew he'd gone out.

He walked through town, sticking to side streets for the shade of the huge trees that lined them. Also, if he were honest, it was to avoid bumping into Caralee. He figured she was out there somewhere, driving around, policing her quiet township.

She was an interesting character. If he'd met her off duty somewhere, he probably would have never pegged her for a cop. That was likely more of a statement of his own bias than any reflection on her professionalism. After meeting her a few times now, he knew she was all about the job. She took her role very seriously, even if she had assured him she'd much rather let her grandfather step back into his old shoes as police chief.

It made perfect sense to Will that the Sergeant Billings who had caused so much trouble for him last night hadn't respected Caralee's authority. He probably resented a female being put in a position of authority over him—he seemed the type to have that kind of archaic mentality. Will just wished he hadn't let the guy push his buttons so easily. He thought he'd grown beyond such childish antics, but apparently some things still got to him.

Being accused of criminal behavior was obviously one of them.

He supposed he'd have to get used to it, though. With his record, what was everyone to think? He could explain his past until he was blue in the face, but who was going to believe him? Would Caralee? She had access to his file, and she would have read up on his case. What could he say that might convince her he'd been wrongly convicted?

Then again, why did it matter? She was no one to him—just somebody helping him out in a tight spot... and doing so very reluctantly. Once he got back into his house, he'd finish his work, then be out of Blossom Township and never think about it again.

Or the redheaded acting police chief who sometimes forgot to hide the hint of sympathy in her smile. Or was it pity?

He rounded a corner onto Maple Street and grinned when his house came into view. It still had a long way to go before it looked good, but he'd gotten a lot done already. He was proud of his work. Maybe some bad things had come from the path his life had taken, but he would always be grateful for the construction skills he'd learned since his teen years. The man who taught him might've been a hypocrite and a cheat, but he had given Will a trade. Whatever direction Will went from here, those skills would serve him well, and he knew it.

With no one in sight, he walked confidently up his driveway. Yellow caution tape surrounded the house and the imposing garden gate with words that read Police Line—Do Not Cross. He hoped he wouldn't have to.

As he neared the house, it struck him as odd that the tape across the front door was placed so haphazardly. He hadn't been here when the investigators had put it up, but would they really have been so lax? It hung slack over the doorway.

Had someone been inside, other than police? He'd been forced to leave his house key with Caralee so the teams could gain access. Had they not locked up? Could someone have taken advantage of his absence to get in? He had thousands of dollars' worth of tools in there! His entire life was wrapped up in this house. If those cops had allowed someone to steal from him, or destroy his hard work…

He leaped up onto the porch and grabbed the door handle. Locked. Well, that was a good sign. Still worried, he peered in through the front window. It was quite a relief to see his tools there, where he had left them midjob. Or were they?

He pressed his face closer to the pane, confused by what he saw. The nice square gauge he had just bought was on the floor, leaning at an odd angle as if it had simply been dropped there. He wouldn't have left it like that—he valued his tools too much. And what about his chop saw? It appeared to have been left in the open position, not carefully shut and latched. He was sure he hadn't done that, either.

The more he scanned the interior of his house, the more little things he noticed. Tools were out of place, boxes of nails were scattered on the floor instead of carefully stacked on the counter. Was this what crime scene investigators did? Messed up people's belongings for no good reason? He hadn't even been told they'd been through the house. Caralee had indicated their work had been in the backyard, recovering the body. Investigation inside his home was still to be done, as far as he knew.

He silently fumed. It had to be the investigators—

anyone else would have stolen things or trashed the place even worse. From what he could see from here at the window, someone had simply been inside, moving things around. The cops were probably looking for something.

A rustling sound from under the porch caught his attention. *Movement.* He could hear soft sounds, someone whimpering. It was clear he wasn't alone.

Good. Hopping over the side of the porch, Will dropped down to sit on the smooth, weathered rock that must've been decorating that corner of the front landscaping for ages. He slipped off the backpack and dropped it into the weeds beside him. As he slid his foot under the porch where some of the decorative lattice was broken, his work boot clanged on something metal. He reached in and pulled out the shiny silver bowl that had been tucked under there. It was bone dry.

"Come on, Bruno," he called. "Here's some fresh water, and I brought you some food."

A nervous whine from under the porch assured him that his little friend was still there. He hoped the poor guy hadn't felt too abandoned with Will being gone overnight. Not that Bruno was interactive.

Will had only been here for two days when the puppy appeared. He looked to be some sort of beagle mix, maybe five or six months old. And he was underweight and dehydrated. The poor little guy was thrilled with the food and water Will started leaving out for him, but he was so shy he'd never come close enough for Will to pet him or check him over to see what other issues he might have.

His hope was that over time the pup would grow to

trust him. Being banished from the house this way, Will worried that whatever steps forward he'd made would be erased. With strangers traipsing around, searching for long-lost evidence, little Bruno would undoubtedly be frightened. It was quite a relief to know he hadn't run off.

"Here you go. It's still nice and cool for you," Will said, pulling out the thermos.

He poured water into the bowl, then crawled partly through the gap in the lattice to put the bowl closer to Bruno. There wasn't much light filtering through the porch, but just enough to see the sad little dog about ten feet away from him. He wiggled his scrawny body in excitement, happy to see a friendly face, but still not confident enough to creep closer.

"It's okay. Here you go, boy," Will said, retrieving the old plate he'd left under the porch.

Pulling the plastic baggie from his backpack, he dumped his leftover lunch onto the plate. Usually he gave Bruno two meals a day of the best brand of puppy food he could afford. But that was sealed up in the house right now, and Will's grocery money was locked in his truck at the police impound lot. For now, Bruno would have to make do with half of Will's lunch.

The puppy sniffed the air and eyed him warily, inching forward. He had to be hungry, so it didn't take long for his fear of Will to be overridden by the tempting scent of the casserole. Will backed up just a bit, and Bruno dove in. He ate in big gulps.

"Slow down, you'll choke yourself." Will laughed, watching the white tip on Bruno's tail flop back and forth in appreciation. Maybe this little dog wasn't such a hopeless case, after all. Maybe eventually he'd let Will lure him out from under the porch to run around and play like a normal puppy should feel safe enough to do.

Will was smiling at the thought of it when a voice called his name from behind. He jolted in surprise, banging his head on a beam under the porch. He knew that voice.

Caralee. She was here, and from the sound of it, not at all happy to find him crawling around under his porch. Her timing could not have been worse.

Bruno yelped and scurried into a dark corner. Will bit back an angry exclamation and pulled himself out into the daylight. Sure enough, Caralee glared down at him.

"I thought you understood this place is off-limits!"

"I'm not crossing any police lines here," he grumbled, rising to stand and dust the dirt off his jeans. "I haven't gone in the house or in the backyard or anything."

"Right…you were just crawling under the porch. Seriously, Will, I hoped I could trust you, but I guess I can't. What were you retrieving down there?"

"Nothing," he replied, confused by the question.

"Okay, then, what were you hiding down there?"

"I wasn't hiding anything."

He waved his hands to show they were empty, but in the process he dislodged the plastic bag he'd stuffed back in his pocket. It fluttered to the ground at Caralee's feet. She stared at it, then looked back at him.

"What was in the bag, Will?"

Her suspicions cut him. What did she think he'd been doing? He instantly went on the defensive. "It's nothing that concerns you."

"This is a crime scene. Everything that goes on here concerns me. What was in the bag? Did you…did you bring it from my grandfather's house? Did you take something from there and hide it under your porch to collect it later?"

"Of course not! Yes, I brought the bag from his house, but I wasn't hiding anything."

She looked positively furious. "I knew inviting you out there was a mistake. Whatever you stole from my grandfather, I want it back. You go right back under that porch and get it."

"Um… I can't."

"You most certainly can, and you'd better! Don't make this any worse for yourself, Will."

"I'm sorry, but I can't. Bruno ate it already."

She blinked in angry confusion. *"Bruno?"*

He nodded his head toward the porch. "He's under there."

She went quiet for a moment. Before he could explain things, she shoved him aside, pulled a flashlight off her belt and crouched down to peer under the porch. Will could see the light flickering through the lattice as she shone the beam around. Suddenly, it stopped moving.

"There's a dog under here," Caralee announced.

"That's Bruno. I brought him some of my lunch."

She turned to glare up at him. *"That's* what you took from my grandfather's house? *Lunch?"*

"Yeah. He needs to eat, and his dog food is locked inside the house."

"He looks terrible."

"Well, he's a stray."

"He looks hungry."

"He *is* hungry. I've been feeding him for a couple weeks, trying to convince him that people aren't as scary as he thinks they are. I'm pretty sure you're not helping my cause."

She clicked off her flashlight and stood back up to face him. "So he just lives under the porch here?"

"It's the only place he feels safe."

"*This* is the reason you wanted me to bring you back here earlier, isn't it?"

"There's no one else to look after him."

"You could have told me about him!"

"Why, so you would call your dog warden to come throw him in a cage, like you did to me?"

She gave a frustrated sigh. Will mentally kicked himself for letting his anger show…again. Insulting Caralee wouldn't serve any good purpose, yet here he was, bickering with her again.

"I'm sorry, Will. I shouldn't have assumed you were up to no good. But seriously, you should have told me about this! I could have helped out, and…"

Her gaze caught on something behind him, and her words faded out. Will turned to find a car pulling up on the street in front of the house. An older man in a business suit stepped out. He smiled at Caralee, then waved. Will glanced at her to see that her reaction to the man was a whole lot more cheerful than it had been toward him.

"Hey, Caralee! What a pleasant surprise to find you here," the man called, walking toward them.

"Mr. Fields, it's nice to see you. What are you up to today?" she asked with a warm smile that she certainly had never turned Will's way.

"Looking for business, of course," the man said.

Will didn't like him. Maybe it wasn't right to make such snap judgments, but he knew a wheeler-dealer when he saw one. Whatever business this guy was looking for, Will was pretty sure Caralee didn't know about it.

"I should have guessed," she said with a lighthearted chuckle. "Do you know Will Viveners?"

"Not yet, but I was hoping to find him," the man said, thrusting his hand forward as if he and Will were about to become lifelong friends. "It's good to meet you."

Will shook his hand out of courtesy.

"This is D.R. Fields," Caralee said by way of introduction. "He's got the biggest real estate office here in Blossom Township. When you're ready to sell, he's the one you'll want to represent you."

Will wanted to extract his hand even quicker now that he had that bit of information, but the man was shaking it heartily and making intense eye contact that was probably supposed to make Will think he could be trusted. It didn't work.

"Call me D.R.," the man said. "Caralee and I go way back. She's practically family!"

Will finally got his hand back. He absently brushed it off on his jeans. "Practically family, huh?"

D.R. grinned. "She was real close with my son, Tad. He had such a crush on her! You two went to the senior prom together, didn't you, Caralee? Homecoming king and queen, too. Tad will be back in town for the summer in fact, working remotely for that big firm he's with. I know he's looking forward to seeing you again."

"It'll be great to catch up," Caralee said.

Will didn't like D.R., and as he watched Caralee

smile about this Tad person coming back to town, Will was pretty sure he didn't like him, either. Caralee's homecoming king was probably just as shady as his father. An intelligent, caring, gorgeous woman like Caralee could surely do better than whoever Tad was.

Not that it was Will's place to think of her that way.

Chapter Six

Caralee inwardly cringed at D.R.'s words. She was trying to remain professional, to present herself with credibility and authority. It didn't help to have her childhood friend's dad making jokes about past crushes and senior proms.

"What business brings you over here today, D.R.?" Caralee asked, hoping to redirect the conversation. "As you can see, this is a crime scene. If it's Will you want to talk to, you'll have to meet up with him elsewhere."

"Oh, I heard about the crime scene," D.R. said, his gaze scanning eagerly over the yellow police tape. "It's big news around town, of course. They say you found someone who's been plant food for a long, long time here. But you probably can't talk about it, can you?"

"No, we can't."

D.R. nodded and craned his neck to survey the broken lattice around the base of the porch. He must have noticed them peering under there as he drove up. For whatever reason, it interested him.

"Were you guys looking for clues under there?" he asked.

"No," she answered quickly.

He laughed. "And of course if you were, you couldn't talk about it, right?"

"Right. So, what can we do for you, D.R.?"

"Oh… I came over to tell Mr. Viveners how impressed I am with all the work he's done on this place. It's looking really good, Will."

"Um, thanks," Will said, glancing over at Caralee with a confused look.

He was clearly surprised by D.R.'s flattery. Caralee was a bit surprised by it, too. Not that Will hadn't made great progress here, but she was surprised D.R. had noticed. Of course he kept a close eye on real estate around town, but from what Caralee had seen, he usually focused on the more high-end properties. Mrs. Viveners's old house was nice—or would be again someday—but it didn't seem like anything that would catch D.R.'s attention.

Will really must know a thing or two about the renovations he was doing, if D.R. had taken note. If anyone recognized quality work, it was him. He must be really impressed with Will. Too bad she'd have to warn him later about Will's checkered past.

"I guess this crime business is going to slow down your progress," D.R. said to Will. "What's your plan for the property? Thinking about staying in the area?"

"No," Will replied. He sounded perfectly sure of that answer. "I'll be selling once I'm done with the renovation."

"Ah," D.R. said thoughtfully.

Caralee half expected him to dive into a sales pitch right there, getting Will signed up as a client with his brokerage, but he didn't. Instead, he just studied the house. He gave special attention, she noticed, to the porch. What was he looking at? Or what was he looking *for*?

"Are you sure there isn't anything we can do for you?" Caralee asked again.

D.R. shook his head, bringing his attention back to her. "No, no, I was just passing by... Don't look now, but I think we're being spied on."

He inclined his head toward the house next door. Will frowned, but Caralee glanced past him. Sure enough, there was a face peering out of a window. Caralee recognized it immediately.

She waved. "Hello, Mrs. Petosky!"

The woman seemed startled to realize she'd been seen, but she waved back meekly. Caralee smiled. She hadn't seen the woman for several years now. It was good to know she was still the same old busybody she used to be.

"You know her?" Will asked.

"Jewel Petosky. She's lived there forever. I used to see her when I'd come visit Mrs. Viveners. I should probably go over and talk to her."

"Good luck with that," Will muttered.

"Well, I guess I should be off," D.R. said, suddenly losing interest. "Keep up the good work here, Will. I mean, once you can get back to it. Caralee, it's great seeing you. I'll have Tad give you a call when he's back, okay?"

"Sure, Mr. Fields. Looking forward to it."

D.R. smiled at her, nodded toward Will and shot one

quick glance at Mrs. Petosky in her window. It only lasted a moment, but Caralee was certain his expression went darker, just for that time. Did he have something against Mrs. Petosky? She couldn't imagine what.

"So his son Tad is your ex, huh?" Will asked as soon as D.R. was out of earshot.

"What? No, Tad and I hung out a lot, but it wasn't serious. I certainly don't call him my *ex*, or anything like that."

"Somebody else gets that distinction?"

"As a matter of fact, I… I don't think that's any of your business."

She tried to seem aloof, but he just gave her another of his mischievous grins. Apparently, Will Viveners liked to push her buttons. Well, she would be more careful not to let him get to her. Any personal life she might—or might not—have was no concern of his.

"Don't tell me you're 'all about the job,' Chief. No time for a social life?"

"I *am* all about the job, thank you. I came over here to check on the site and make sure it was still secure."

"As you can see, I haven't disturbed it."

"Except that I found you crawling around under the porch."

"Yeah, and you know exactly what I was doing under there, too. But why did the local con man show up? That seems like the question you ought to be asking."

"He's in real estate," she reminded him. "He was probably looking to drum up some legitimate business, make sure you list with him when you're ready to sell."

Will nodded. "Yeah, maybe."

"He said as much. You don't believe him?"

"Not as far as I can throw him."

"And you grumbled about Mrs. Petosky, too. What's your problem with her?"

"Who said I have a problem with her?"

"Do you distrust everyone, or is something up with her?"

"I don't have a problem with her," he said. "How can I? She won't even look at me. Sure, she spies out her window all day, but the minute I try to be neighborly, she pulls the curtains and hides. I tried knocking on the door to introduce myself, but she wouldn't answer, even though I'd just seen her at the window."

"She's elderly. She might be nervous around strangers."

"If she'd answer her door and talk to me, I wouldn't be a stranger."

"Well, maybe she'll talk to me. I need to get interviews from all the close neighbors. Maybe someone remembers something that might help find out who was buried here and why."

He seemed doubtful. "You really think anyone knows anything? Why wouldn't they have come forward in all this time?"

"The only way to find out is to ask. I'll start with Mrs. Petosky, and I'll have a couple officers come out to canvass the area later on."

"Good idea. And hey…if you do get to speak with Mrs. Petosky, um…"

"Yeah?"

"Just let her know she doesn't need to be scared of me. As long as we're neighbors here, she ought to feel comfortable in her own home, right?"

"Sure. I'll let her know."

She had to admit, it was awfully nice of Will to think about the little old lady next door. Most guys would just ignore her, but Will really seemed to care.

She hoped Jewel would open the door for her. Not only would it be nice to see her again, but maybe she could set the woman's mind at ease regarding her new neighbor.

Will wasn't so bad. Rough around the edges, that was for sure, but Caralee believed he'd never cause any trouble for Jewel. Maybe she'd even hire him for some odd jobs or something. If Will had earned D.R.'s approval, perhaps he could pick up extra cash as a handyman while he waited to get back to work on his own place.

Caralee wasn't quite ready to vouch for him yet, but if things went okay at Grandpa's house over the next couple days, she might. Will seemed the kind of guy who liked to be busy, and if she could drum up some work for him, at least she wouldn't have to wonder what he was getting up to.

She left Will at his house and started up the driveway toward Jewel's front door, but a flicker of light caught her eye. Will must've gone back under the porch to check on that stray dog. She could see his flashlight through the lattice and the weedy overgrowth. It was great that he wanted to help the poor thing, but clearly occasional leftovers and a bottle of water now and then was not enough. The dog needed proper care and probably a checkup at the vet. She knew Will wouldn't be happy about it, but truly the best thing to do would be to call the dog warden. If the dog was as skittish as

Will said, it might take a whole team of humane officers to capture him.

Pausing to focus on Will's porch again, she peered through the neglected plantings to investigate the condition of the porch lattice. She'd seen the broken area on the other side. Was the rest of it secure enough to act as a barricade to keep the puppy confined? The warden would want to know what he'd be dealing with when he came to collect the dog.

The wooden slats of the lattice that lined the underside of the porch were old and warped. A bigger, more confident dog would probably have no difficulty breaking through it. The puppy, however, didn't seem to realize he could even try. She reached out and grabbed the lattice to give it a cautious shake. It rattled as pieces shifted and rusted tacks came loose.

A yelp came from nearby, just under the porch. There were sounds of scrambling paws in the dank dirt. Caralee jumped back. The puppy must have been hiding right there, where she was testing the lattice. She'd startled the poor little thing, and now he was making a daring escape.

"Hey!" Will called out from the other side.

There were more footsteps and shuffling in the dirt under the porch. Caralee frowned, picturing the sad little pup tearing through the lattice in fear and running away. It would be twice as hard to help him now if she had spooked him.

"Sorry," she said, jogging back toward Will. "I didn't realize I was so close to him. Did I chase him off?"

Will was just emerging from under the porch. To her surprise, he held the shaking puppy in his arms.

They were both muddy and covered in cobwebs, but Will wore a grin.

"He came running right to me! I guess he figured between the two of us, I was the safer one."

"Poor little guy! I didn't mean to scare him."

"Everything scares him. Whatever you did, though, was the right thing. He practically leaped into my arms while I was under there refilling his water bowl—I couldn't believe it. This is the first time he's let me touch him!"

"He still looks pretty nervous. I'm worried he might squirm away and bolt."

"Yeah, I wish I had some safe place to put him."

"My car."

"Your *police* car?"

"Don't worry, I'm sure no one will assume he's a criminal if they see him in there."

"No, they'll do that just by seeing him with me."

She laughed at his self-deprecating humor as she led the way back to her car. "Come on, I'll unlock the door."

"Are you sure about this? He hasn't exactly had a bath in…well, ever."

"As long as he's not as bad as two drunks on a three-day bender, he won't be the worst mess I've had in there."

"Yuck."

"Yeah. It's a glamorous job. Here you go."

She opened the door to the back seat of her cruiser. The puppy wriggled, but Will held him fast. Once in the confines of the car, it wouldn't be so hard to control him. Will hesitated before hopping in, though. Caralee realized this might not be the easiest thing for him to do. He'd already been in and out of cop cars too many times in less than twenty-four hours.

"He's going to need you to help calm him," she said softly. "Do you mind sitting back there with him?"

"No handcuffs this time?" he asked. His grin was supposed to convey his usual tone of carefree teasing, but she was getting to know him well enough to recognize the hint of vulnerability behind it all. He was doing this for the puppy, but he didn't like it.

"No handcuffs," she promised. "For either of you."

"Good," he muttered. "Bruno hates them."

"It's going to be okay, boy," Will soothed when he and Bruno were situated in the back of the cruiser.

He wasn't terribly comfortable there himself, and Bruno was shaking like a leaf. It was actually a relief when Caralee announced she'd put off her attempt to interview Mrs. Petosky.

"I think it's best to get this puppy someplace safe," she said. "He looks about as thrilled to be here as you do. I can come back later."

"So where are we going to take him?" Will asked.

He wasn't sure he wanted to hear the answer. Even as skittish as he was, Will had come to enjoy his little interactions with the puppy. It had felt good to buy a bag of puppy food for him. Such a normal thing to do, but something that he hadn't even dreamed of just a few months ago. He would miss his shy little buddy once Bruno was delivered to a shelter or vet somewhere.

Caralee backed the car slowly out onto the street, but clearly the noise of the engine bothered the dog. Will held him tightly, and Bruno buried his head under Will's arm. For all they knew, this could be the poor dog's first car ride. Will could only hope he wouldn't regret it.

"We'll just take him home, if that's okay," Caralee replied.

For a moment, Will was confused. "Home?"

"To my grandfather's house. That's your home right now, isn't it?"

"Yes, but…"

"You don't mind taking care of him for a while longer, do you?"

"No! If you're okay with me keeping him there, I'm happy to look after him."

"Good. He seems to like you, and I happen to know the shelter is overcrowded right now."

"Your grandfather won't mind?"

"He loves dogs! Besides, he knows I've got a crime scene to protect and investigate. I can't spend all day calling around to find a dog a foster home, and I certainly can't leave the little guy there to dig up any of our clues."

"I guess that's true. So you'll be active in the investigation? It's not just handed over to the CSI team?"

"This is a police case, being in the township limits. I'm the one coordinating the various units involved. The sheriff is supplying some manpower, and of course the state is involved, too, but my officers and I will handle the interviews in the neighborhood."

"Yeah…sorry Bruno interrupted you talking to that nosy neighbor. As much as she likes to spy on people, if she's lived here a while she might actually know something. Any idea yet how long that body was buried?"

"No, but as you saw, there's not much left of it. It's probably been there a decade or more."

"It was pretty gruesome, for sure. You don't think… it might have been there a couple decades? Or maybe three?"

Will watched Caralee's reaction. Her brow creased as she understood what he was asking. She hesitated to speak, then shook her head.

"You think this might be…your *father*? No, it can't be. Whoever it is must have been buried here long before the Viveners moved in."

"The lawyers said it's been in the family two generations already. So who put the body there?"

"Well, not Mrs. Viveners. She was like a timid little granny! She baked cookies and we had tea parties in her garden. I don't know how the body got there, but Mrs. Viveners didn't do it. Maybe someone took advantage of the privacy she had with that high fence. Maybe a worker she hired at some point—who knows?"

"So you don't think…well, she *was* married to my father, and he *was* obviously cheating on her before he disappeared nearly thirty years ago. You really don't think—"

Caralee cut him off quickly. "I think we shouldn't speculate until we have more information. When we know more, then we'll have theories. Until then, don't chew yourself up, Will. Don't assume the worst."

"Okay, but at some point we'll have to ask ourselves how Mrs. Viveners let a complete stranger end up buried in her secret garden."

"And that's exactly what I'm going to find out."

"Better you than me." He chuckled, shaking off his dark concerns. "Seems like quite a tough job you've got. Whoever the dead guy is, if no one's been looking for him all this time, maybe no one really cares that he's gone."

"Well, someone cared enough to put him—or her—there in the first place. I just need to figure out who it was."

Chapter Seven

Will patiently held the treat out for Bruno. The nervous puppy was doing a combination of tail wagging and cowering. It was sad to see the poor little thing so eager to be a puppy, but still so full of fear. He nearly cheered out loud when Bruno finally got brave enough to inch forward and take the treat from his hand.

"That's a good boy!" he encouraged softly. The tail wagging continued, and Bruno only took two timid steps backward as he quickly gulped down the treat.

He looked really cute in the bright red plaid collar Caralee had found for him. The matching leash hung slack at his side. Getting them on the squirming little guy after his bath had been a challenge, but he seemed at ease with them now. So far, this second day of being domesticated was going pretty well for the little dog.

It wasn't so bad for Will, either. He was finding it quite comfortable here in the elder police chief's big house. They'd arrived back here with Bruno yesterday afternoon after stopping on the way to pick up more puppy food and some training treats. Will assured Caralee he had plenty in his house, but she insisted on getting more.

Bruno didn't particularly enjoy his first car ride, and it was all Will could do to keep a grip on him when they finally arrived at the house. Will was overjoyed when Caralee had opened a cupboard to reveal a whole supply of dog items—collars, leashes, dishes for food and water. Her grandfather had kept everything after his own beloved mutt, Scout, had passed away last year.

Will had been thrilled to find there was even a bottle of dog shampoo. Bruno had needed that badly. He'd gotten his first bath about five minutes after Caralee left them. Bruno looked great all cleaned up, but Will had needed another shower.

Bruno already seemed more at ease today. Caralee would be impressed by the progress they'd made. She hadn't stayed long yesterday, just dropped them off then headed back to talk to Jewel Petosky. Apparently, Caralee worked on weekends, even if the crime scene investigators didn't. Will wondered what she had learned. Had Jewel been keeping any secrets all these years? Had she even been willing to talk to Caralee?

A car engine sounded nearby, and Bruno jumped. They were outside in the big, fenced backyard, but Will had the dog's leash firmly in hand. He'd made the mistake of letting Bruno out to run around yesterday, and the puppy had immediately gone to hide under a bush. It seemed Bruno only felt safe if he was hiding, so Will kept him tethered, hoping the dog could get used to following Will and feeling safe out in the open. They were doing training now in the shade under a big maple tree.

"It's okay, Bruno," Will soothed. "I promise you're

safe here. And I'm pretty sure there isn't a body buried in *this* backyard."

He chuckled at the irony of it all. For so many years, he'd dreamed of living in a house just like this—having a big yard for kids to play in, smiling photos of loving family on the walls and even a floppy-eared dog ready for a game of fetch. For a brief time he'd thought that life was within reach—it had felt so close. But it hadn't been real. Everything Will thought was a blessing had turned out to be nothing but lies.

The biggest lie of all had been telling himself he could keep on pretending. He couldn't, so it had all come crashing down. Now the only thing he'd been looking forward to was a future that didn't include interaction with law enforcement. And look where he'd ended up! He was stuck living in a police chief's dream house with a murder investigation in his literal backyard.

A murder investigation that could very well lead to his father. Even if it didn't, this was not the happy ending Will had always wished for.

Caralee had assured him she didn't think old Mrs. Viveners had murdered his father. He appreciated her attempt to ease his worries, but who else could that body belong to? He'd be a fool not to acknowledge the possibility.

Yet he was conflicted. A part of him wanted to believe his father hadn't been murdered. But another part yearned to know the man hadn't abandoned them intentionally. Perhaps he wasn't a bad man; maybe they would have had the life and family Will had always longed for. Murder had probably just gotten in the way.

Whichever scenario it was, Will needed to know. Was that his father's body he had uncovered?

First things first. Tomorrow, he'd try to get his truck out of the impound. How much would that cost? His budget was rapidly depleting. It was great he had a free place to stay now, but anything he'd saved by not going to a hotel that first night would be spent on getting his truck back. What a waste.

It was the story of his life, though. Every time it seemed he might be moving ahead, something always happened to set things back again. He shouldn't even be surprised by it anymore, he supposed. If there truly was a God, he certainly seemed to have it in for him.

Will held out another treat for Bruno, but something distracted the dog and he whimpered, tugging the leash to try to hide again. Will realized he'd heard something, too. A car was turning into the driveway.

Scooping Bruno up into his arms, he walked around the side of the house. A red sedan Will didn't recognize was there. He almost didn't recognize the smartly dressed woman who got out of it, either.

"Caralee?"

"Good morning, Will. How's Bruno today?" she asked, coming toward them.

He let her in through the gate, and she gently patted the shivering dog.

"He's taking treats from me, finally. We're not ready to go off leash yet, though."

"Slow progress is still progress," she said. "At least you got the fleas and mud off him. He looks great!"

"Who knew he had so much white fur?" Will chuckled. "I'm just hoping he'll forgive me for this bath before it's time for his next one."

"He will. Dogs forgive a lot easier than people do."

"That's for sure. So, what brings you here this morning? And what's with the fancy clothes?"

She frowned and glanced down at her outfit. "What? Oh, believe it or not, I don't wear that uniform every day. I'm just on my way to church now."

"Right, it's Sunday. I hope I'm not expected to go with you. That's not part of the deal, is it?"

"No, you made your feelings about church very clear. I won't drag you with me."

"Good."

"You'd be welcome, though."

"I'll pass. Thanks."

"Maybe next week."

"I plan to be back in my house continuing renovations at this time next week," he declared. "Any idea if that will be possible?"

He put Bruno back on the ground. At first, the dog tugged the leash in an effort to dash into the nearest corner, but then something caught his attention, and he started sniffing the ground. It was the first time Will had seen him let his guard down so quickly. That was a good sign.

"Well… I don't know," Caralee replied. "The team is supposed to get in there tomorrow. I'm not sure how soon they'll be done."

"What is there to do?" Will asked. "I can't imagine there will be any clues left after all this time. Didn't they already send the body to a big crime lab somewhere?"

"Yes, but we can't risk overlooking something. The

team needs to make a thorough inspection of the property, inside and out."

"And they haven't done that?" he asked, thinking about the mislaid tools he'd noticed yesterday.

She shook her head. "No, the team only had time on Friday to focus on retrieving the body. That's why it's been so important to keep the site contained over the weekend."

"Hmm, and you're sure you've been able to do that?"

"Well, aside from you crawling around under the porch, I'm not aware of anything happening there. Why do you ask?"

"It's just that the tape over the front door looked kind of…tampered with. And when I looked in the front windows—"

"You were looking in the windows?"

"It's my house! I've got some expensive tools in there, and I was worried."

"Was everything okay when you looked in?"

"It was all there, I think," he said. "But it wasn't the way I'd left it. Things were moved around…kind of carelessly, too."

She frowned, and he liked the way her mouth quirked up to one side in serious contemplation. It was nice to know she didn't instantly dismiss his concerns. He'd half thought she might.

"There was no one in there, not to my knowledge," she assured him. "But if you say things weren't as you left them—"

"They weren't."

"I'll look into it. Maybe the sheriff sent someone in and just forgot to tell me. I'll find out, Will, but you need to promise me you won't go back over there. Especially if someone has been tampering with the site. I need to know you aren't involved. Can you promise me?"

He met her eyes. They were such a deep blue, almost endless in color. They were earnestly searching his eyes, too. She wanted to trust him—he could see that. She just didn't believe she could.

He wanted more than anything to convince her.

"Yeah. I promise, Caralee. I'll stay away."

"Thanks." Her smile was more than a reward.

"Good. We'll get this. You'll get back into your house and we'll find our answers."

"Thanks," he said, taking a step away from her to avoid falling into those deep blue eyes of hers. "I've been thinking of how I can help out with that."

"We've got teams from three separate law enforcement entities," she said. "Plus state-of-the-art resources."

"But you don't have my DNA."

"DNA?"

"To help identify the body."

"Will, we're not sure this *is* your father. It could be anyone."

"Anyone who used to live in that house, who cheated on his wife and who disappeared thirty years ago."

"But I talked to Jewel last night," she said quickly. "She's as surprised by this as everyone. She was adamant that Violet Viveners could not have killed her husband. In fact, she assured me that Violet occasionally heard from the man for years after he went missing. I'm sorry, Will, but it seems like the story you heard all your life is true—he simply abandoned *both* of his families."

"Jewel actually talked to you?"

"Yes, and she was Violet's closest friend. She would've known if Violet killed someone. In fact, maybe that body has been there even longer than we think."

"How long?"

Now she paused before answering. "Well…as you mentioned, the house was in your father's family before he came to own it. I did some searching online. His parents sold the house to him when they retired. He already owned it when he married Violet."

"So you're saying…maybe my father murdered someone and buried them in the backyard?"

"I'm not saying anything, because we don't know anything yet."

"We know there was a dead body in that garden, and someone obviously put it there a long time ago. Since you don't think my father could be the victim, he must be the murderer. After all, he is *my* father, right?"

"Will, I'm not saying that."

The transition from thinking that his father could be a victim to considering that he could be a murderer was too much for Will. No, he couldn't accept it as a possibility. He'd already been abandoned, betrayed, cast aside by people he should have looked up to. He'd tried to convince himself he was better than that, prayed he could rise above it, that he might be a better person than those who had hurt him. Now he was expected to accept that his father—his own flesh and blood—could be a murderer on top of everything?

He couldn't let himself go there.

"I get it, Caralee. My father wasn't around to defend himself. It was easy to let him play the role of bad guy year after year. Meanwhile, everyone loved Violet Viveners, so obviously she—"

"No, everyone did *not* love her!" she interrupted. "She was a recluse, didn't have many friends at all. She was worse than Jewel."

"What about your tea parties in her garden?"

"My mother was on the church visiting committee. It was her duty to visit the homebound, so that's why she came to see Violet. The only reason she brought me along was because I was a cute little kid and Violet didn't have the heart to slam the door in my face. Mom was the only church lady she ever let into the garden. I didn't know how rare that was until I got older, but as a child I just thought Violet was this nice old lady with a beautiful garden. By that time, she'd come to enjoy our visits. I felt sorry for her, so I kept coming and let her tell me all about her garden. She really had some amazing flowers there, you know. She won awards every year at the North Shore Flower Show."

"That's a big thing? I've seen posters about it around town."

"Yeah. Our local garden club is quite competitive, and only a select few get chosen to go on to the flower show. That garden club was the only activity Violet was involved in outside her home, and from what I've heard, the club only tolerated her because her flowers won awards."

"That tangled, overgrown mess won awards?" He had a hard time believing that. In all his work pulling up weeds and battling crabgrass out there, he hadn't seen evidence of many flowers.

"Her daylily seedlings were famous, as a matter of fact. She registered a new one just about every year."

"What happened to it all?"

Caralee shrugged. "Well, after she passed, the garden club members were tripping over themselves to get in there. At first, they looked after the place, fighting over which one of them was going to buy the house and take over the garden."

"Why didn't anyone buy it?"

"Because it was still in your father's name. So it just sat there while lawyers for the estate searched for him. I guess little by little, the people looking after the garden felt it would be easier to look after things if they dug them up and took them home."

"So all those prize-winning flowers are in someone else's garden now?"

"That's what people say. I know Violet kept careful records of things, but who knows where they are now? Every now and then I think I see some of her daylilies blooming around town, but there's no way to prove it. Sorry, but I don't think you'll be able to get any of them back."

"It figures. I suppose award-winning flowers are valuable?"

"No, not really," she said. "Bragging rights, mostly. Although there was one new daylily Violet was getting ready to introduce. She said there was a big wholesaler interested in it, and she thought there might be some money in making a deal with them."

"Who ended up making the deal?"

"No one. I've never seen that flower again. I don't think anyone else even knew about it, actually."

"So they wouldn't have known to save it. It probably just died off, I suppose."

"Daylilies are pretty hardy," she said. "It could be there, hidden in the mess. Unless you already ripped it out without knowing it."

"That does seem like the way things usually go for me." He sighed. "I don't have time to sort through every leaf and root out there. I'll probably just dig the whole thing out and put in sod. Whoever buys the place won't want a bunch of fussy old plants to look after anyway."

"Maybe if you find remnants of Violet's beautiful plants, a local person will pay extra."

"You think?"

"Maybe. It was a beautiful garden. Such a shame to just sod over everything if there's even a chance you could save it. I hope you'll at least think about it."

"And thinking about it is all I can do right now. But I'm holding you up. Aren't you going to be late for church?"

She paused and checked her watch. Then she chewed her lower lip before replying. "I'm still good. I just came by to…well, I keep thinking about yesterday. I need to tell you I'm sorry."

"For what?"

"First of all, I'm sorry that when I showed up at your house and saw you crawling under the porch, I automatically assumed you were up to something. I shouldn't have done that—you've given me no reason to accuse you of anything, yet I did. I owe you an apology for that."

He was definitely caught off guard. He wasn't used to apologies. Certainly not ones delivered in person.

"Um, that's okay. You were just doing your job."

She wouldn't let him off that easily. She shook her

head, and her gingery curls bounced in the sunlight. "No, my job isn't to think the worst of people, and that's what I did. Then when I brought you and Bruno back here afterward, I don't think I told you how nice the place looks."

"Sure you did. You noticed I got all the mowing done."

"You did a great job. You even did the trimming, and I know Grandpa would be impressed. I was in a hurry to get back to work, but I should have taken a couple minutes to thank you for going the extra mile. You could have slacked off, but you didn't."

He knew she didn't mean for her words to hurt him, but they did. She had expected so little of him! But of course, there wasn't much to expect. He was such an obvious failure that any small accomplishment must come as a surprise. She'd known him for three days, and already she could see it. He was no better than his father before him.

But she was waiting for a response, and he hated to disappoint her. Taking a deep breath, he forced a smile and accepted her apology.

"All right, thank you," he said. "I appreciate you coming by to tell me that. But just so you know, I didn't do the job to get a thank-you. I did the job because I said I would. I keep my word."

"And I just want you to know that I appreciate it. My grandpa will, too. I plan to visit him this afternoon. He'll be glad to hear how you're taking care of things for him."

"I hope knowing his place is in good hands helps him relax."

"It will." She smiled at him. "I've got to go, but…if you can come into the office tomorrow, I'll have someone collect your DNA sample. We can send it off to the lab. You're right—it would be helpful to narrow down the identity of our victim. If it is your father, you deserve to know that."

"And if it isn't?"

"Well, you deserve to know that, too."

Chapter Eight

Caralee smiled at her fellow churchgoers as she made her way out to the center aisle after service was over. It would've been nice if Will could have come. If Will *would* have come, she mentally corrected. It was clear something in his past had left him angry and distrustful of church. As the beautiful strains of the final hymn played in the background, Caralee prayed that God would guide her in any way that might help Will find the healing he needed.

For now, though, she was hoping to hurry over to the hospital. Of course the usual Sunday morning pleasantries had to be exchanged before she could duck out. Most of the people around her had been a part of her life since childhood, and she could hardly ignore their smiles and heartfelt greetings.

Mr. and Mrs. Belamy had been her youth leaders years ago. Now they were retired and spent their winters in Florida. She waved at them. Mark and Brenda Minton had been in high school with her. They were married with two children now. Caralee stepped sideways as their younger child zoomed past her, proudly waving his coloring project from Sunday school. Happy conversation blended with the music that filled the air to create a truly joyful noise.

Once again, she had found hope and encouragement in today's message. It was really too bad Will was so set against church. What could've happened that made him so hard-hearted?

Then again, he'd been very forgiving of her attitude toward him. He'd smiled when she'd been insulting. He'd given her honest answers when he probably would have rather kept silent. And he'd certainly shown real kindness and compassion as he walked all the way back to his house just to help care for a stray puppy. She was glad she'd stopped by this morning to apologize. Her own conscience had been niggling at her all night, and she'd needed to clear the air between them.

Hopefully, they could both be less suspicious of each other as this investigation moved forward.

"So you didn't bring the prisoner with you today?" a voice beside her asked.

Caralee turned to find D.R. Fields filing into line. "I'm sorry, who?" she asked.

"The Viveners guy. Isn't he under house arrest or something?"

"No, he's not. Grandpa invited him to stay at his house while Will's place is designated a crime scene. He's not been arrested."

"Oh, I guess I heard wrong. Well, I'm glad you're keeping an eye on him. He's been in prison, you know."

"Yes, I know all about his record. I'm curious how *you* know about it."

D.R. shrugged. "It's a small town—people talk. Especially when the guy just dug up a corpse in his backyard! So, what's the deal with that? Any news on who it is?"

"You know I can't talk about an ongoing investigation," she replied, very aware that she'd told him the same thing yesterday. "I'll issue a statement when we know something."

"How long will it take? How long is that guy going to be put out of his house?"

"You're eager for him to get back so you can make some kind of deal with him, aren't you?"

"Hey, it's my job."

"Usually the deals you make don't involve half-renovated bungalows on quiet little back streets. What do you see in that place, anyway?"

"It's got charm, and that walled garden is very distinctive. Yeah, maybe I don't usually focus on places like his, but I feel sorry for that guy, and I'm happy to help him out. He seems pretty desperate to sell."

"So that's it. You figure he'll do all that work and you can swoop in and get the place cheap because he's just looking to be rid of it."

"Don't make me sound so callous." D.R. laughed as they passed into the bustling fellowship area outside the sanctuary. "He wants to sell, and I'm happy to help him do that. It's just business."

"I know, but he's had a rough time. Be nice to him."

"Oh, you've got a soft spot for him, do you?"

"What? No... I just don't like to see people being taken advantage of, that's all."

She realized she might have protested too much. *Did*

she have a soft spot for Will? Of course not. Why would she? He was just a good guy in a tough spot. She'd feel the same about anyone; it had nothing to do with Will's broad shoulders and the lopsided smile he gave her when he was teasing.

D.R. merely laughed as her cheeks began to burn. "Fine. I'll be 'nice' to your pet felon. But maybe you'll do something for me in return?"

"What do you mean?"

"Just let me know when you finally *do* learn something, okay? If you find anything…interesting…there at that house. Deal?"

"You think I'm not up to the task? I assure you, D.R., my team will find some answers and we will keep the public informed, okay?"

He shrugged, clearly unimpressed with her promises. "Sure. Just keep an eye on your new buddy."

She didn't like his judgmental tone, but now was not the time to argue with him. Mr. and Mrs. DeBonet were making their way toward her, smiling cheerfully. D.R. noticed and wished her a good day, zipping off toward the wide-open front doors. Caralee sighed and greeted the DeBonets.

"Caralee! I'm so glad you're here today," Geneva DeBonet said brightly. "With that murder investigation, it's a wonder you aren't buried with work."

Her husband, Frank, nudged her and chuckled. "Geneva! Don't talk about the poor girl being *buried*. That's what all this fuss is about to begin with!"

Geneva paused, then laughed when she realized what she'd said. Apparently both DeBonets thought it was hilarious. "Oh! You're right, I shouldn't say *buried*, should

I? Goodness, but who would have ever thought there might be a murder like that here in Blossom Township? Poor Caralee, how are you handling things? We've been thinking of you, all on your own with your grandfather laid up and your parents on that mission trip."

"I'm fine, thank you," she assured them. "It was quite a surprise to find a body, yes, but we've got good people working on it. There's nothing to worry about."

"Good, good. Have you figured out who the poor soul is yet?" Frank asked.

"No, not yet. It will take some time, but we'll release information to the public when we have it."

"Of course," Geneva said. "I don't see how you're keeping up with everything, trying to do your grandfather's job for him while he's down. How is he, the dear man? Has he been able to help you at all with this shocking murder?"

"I have talked to him about it, but right now he needs to rest and concentrate on recovery. I'm handling things, trying not to burden him with it."

"Oh, how sweet. I'm sure the sheriff will know what to do. But is it…is it what people are saying?" Geneva asked, her voice dropping low. "Did Violet murder her husband all those years ago? He was running around with a younger woman, you know."

Caralee realized she'd never heard mention of this before. Her mother never talked about it, Jewel didn't say anything about it, and Violet certainly hadn't, either. All Caralee knew until she met Will was that the elder Mr. Viveners had left his wife. When Will showed up, she assumed Mr. Viveners's second family had been a complete secret. Apparently, it was not.

"You knew about his affair?" Caralee asked.

"We did," Geneva said. "He worked with Frank for a while—they were business partners. When he started running around, well…we knew, but we did *not* approve."

"Not that he deserved to be murdered for it, you understand, but surely it gave Violet a motive," Frank added.

Caralee made sure not to comment on anyone's supposed motive, but she did have a few questions. "I didn't realize it was such common knowledge that he was having an affair. Would you say many people in town knew about it?"

The DeBonets exchanged glances. When Geneva spoke, she was clearly being careful. Caralee appreciated that, but wondered what, exactly, she was being so cautious about all these years later.

"I don't think it was common knowledge," she replied slowly. "Violet knew, of course, but Willard was discreet. I don't believe I ever heard who the young woman was. Did you, Frank?"

"No, he never told me. I just knew he'd met someone and was always looking for excuses to get away to see her."

"Get away? So she wasn't here in Blossom Township?" Caralee asked.

"I don't think so," Frank answered. "He didn't travel much, then all of a sudden it seemed he had business in Cleveland every other weekend. I assumed she lived there, but I have no idea how they met in the first place."

"We get so many tourists," Geneva said. "My guess is she was one of them, just here for a visit, then gone."

"That would certainly explain why no one knew who she was," Caralee said. "Or why she wasn't missed when she ran off with Willard."

"Or why no one spoke up when he disappeared and she didn't," Frank added. "If it's true that *was* his body out there."

"Well, let's be careful about spreading rumors," Caralee reminded him. "Thank you for your information. I may call on you again if I have more questions. Is that okay?"

Frank agreed readily, but Geneva was a little slower to respond. "We are awfully busy these days," she said. "The big flower show is coming up, as you know. Frank and I are always very involved in that."

"Oh, right! It's your busy season, isn't it? I should drive by your house to see all the flowers."

"Stop in if you come by," Frank said. "We'd love to show you around, give you a sneak peek at our future prize winners."

"If we're not too busy, of course," Geneva added. "Come along, Frank. We've got watering to do, and the sun is getting hot today."

Caralee was happy to let them go. In a short time, she'd learned a lot from Frank and Geneva. She needed to ask Will about his mother—what he knew about how she met his father and where she lived at the time. If this did turn out to be Will's father, Geneva had certainly been right about one thing: Willard's affair gave Violet plenty of motive for murder.

As much as Caralee would hate for Will to learn that his father had, indeed, been murdered, it would certainly make solving the crime just a bit easier. She'd have to run all this by Grandpa today and see what he thought. Maybe he had some memories from that time. She didn't want to interrupt his rest, but Geneva had been right. Caralee needed all the help from him she could get.

Will turned the kitchen faucet on and off a few times. The water ran smoothly with no signs of leaking or annoying drips. Good. It had been steadily dripping since he'd gotten here yesterday.

Once he'd completed the bulk of the yard work, he'd searched the house for interior issues to tackle. That drip had been at the top of his list. He was afraid it would need a whole new fixture, but he'd found some fresh washers with the tools, and that seemed to do the trick. Now on to the next little task.

Bruno had finally gotten brave enough to follow Will into the house. He was sleeping comfortably on the floor under the kitchen table, but he startled suddenly. At first Will thought it was because he'd made an unexpected movement, but then he heard the same noise Bruno clearly had.

Someone was coming to the front door. Craning his head around, he could see out into the entryway. A figure passed by the narrow window beside the door. He couldn't tell who it was.

Drying his hands, he dropped the towel onto the counter and headed toward the front door. Instead of a knock, though, there was silence on the other side of the door. Will waited. Maybe whoever it was needed a moment to compose themselves before knocking. He didn't want to startle them by yanking the door open.

Still, nothing.

Finally, he opened the door. It was quite a surprise to find no one there. He did find a letter, though. It had been tucked into the doorjamb. When he opened the door, it fell down onto the welcome mat.

Will picked it up gingerly, then stepped out. He expected to see a car or someone walking away, but there was nothing. Just the same peaceful residential scene that had been there all day. He pulled the door shut behind him and stepped off the porch to get a better view.

The huge sycamore tree in front of the house provided shade but did nothing to obstruct his view. He supposed someone could have ducked around the other side of the garage, but then they would have passed in front of that narrow window again, and he would've seen them. But if they'd gone the other way, the large clump of lilac bushes at the corner of the house would provide cover. Why such secrecy, though? He stepped back inside, perplexed.

Will glanced down at the letter. It was in a plain envelope with just his name on it: *Willard Viveners, Jr.* Someone definitely knew who he was and where he was staying.

He was just about to tear it open when there was a knock at the door. Bruno barked, and Will nearly jumped out of his skin. He was still near the door, so he yanked it open.

"Caralee!"

She smiled and was probably going to speak, but he thrust the letter into her face.

"What is this?" he demanded.

She frowned, leaning back to get a better look at it. "Um, a letter?"

He scanned the yard. No sign of anyone else, and her car was parked in the driveway now. There was no way she could have had time to run off to wherever she might have parked it and then returned. Caralee clearly hadn't delivered the mystery letter.

"Someone just tucked it in my door, then disappeared."

"Just now?"

"Yes," he said. "I heard someone on the porch, then when I opened the door they were gone. No car, nothing. But they left this."

"What does it say?"

"I haven't opened it yet."

"How about if we open it over some dinner?" she suggested, holding up a paper bag with the logo of a local Chinese restaurant on it. "Sweet and sour pork, chicken lo mein, or beef and broccoli?"

"What a nice surprise," he said, taking a deep breath and stepping aside for her to enter. "I didn't expect to see you again today."

"Well, I thought maybe you'd be hungry, so I brought along dinner. I didn't expect disappearing visitors dropping off secret messages."

"Maybe it's just a welcome to the neighborhood." He laughed, ushering her inside. "Here, let's bring the food into the kitchen."

She followed him and put the bag down on the closest countertop. "Okay, now open that letter! You really have no clue who left it?"

"None at all. They've got nice handwriting, though. And they spelled my name correctly."

"You must have a secret admirer."

Will hoped it was as innocent as that, but somehow he didn't think it would be. Taking a knife from the kitchen drawer, he slit the envelope open. Inside was a paper, folded neatly. When he opened that, the same handwriting in the same color ink was inside. He read it twice to make heads or tails of it.

The sins of the father are visited on the children and upon the children's children. Leave Blossom Township before you get what you deserve!

"Wow. I don't even know what to think of this," he said.

"I think it's supposed to be from a Bible verse, but they've badly misquoted it."

"I have a feeling they said exactly what they wanted to say."

"It's a threat," Caralee said. "I can't believe someone left this for you! It's awful. Obviously we're going to investigate this."

"Do you think that's wise?" he questioned.

She seemed surprised by that. "You don't want us to find out who sent it? It's harassment. Someone is obviously trying to terrorize you."

"Well, they're not doing a very good job of it."

"Are you sure?" she asked, and he could hear the concern in her voice. "You're not worried by this?"

"Of course not. If someone wanted to hurt me, I hardly think they'd send me a handwritten note. They'd just show up and, you know, take me out." He held the letter up for her to get another look at. "This is just a lame attempt at getting me to leave."

"So who would want you to leave?"

He shrugged. "That real estate guy wants me to sell, that old biddy in the window clearly doesn't like me making changes to Violet's house, and your old beau Tad is coming back to town. Maybe he doesn't like you bringing me dinner."

"That's ridiculous. None of those people would write this."

"Then maybe your grandfather's neighbors don't like how I cut the grass. Who knows? It's just a stupid letter, and it's not going to work. Maybe some kids did it as a joke."

"Well, it's not very funny."

"Agreed, but I'm not in any imminent danger, so can we bring out the food now? It smells really good, and I'm hungry."

"Fine, but you know I'm not done with this," Caralee announced as she began unpacking the bag of food containers. "That letter is going back to the station with me."

"Careful where you set that, or you'll be taking it back to the station with plum sauce all over it."

Clearly that letter bothered her. She was distracted and nearly spilled their meal. But Will understood; he was also bothered, more than he admitted. True, he didn't believe anyone actually had violence in mind, but the fact that someone had gone to the trouble of writing the letter, then risked being seen delivering it meant they were highly motivated.

But for what? He hadn't been here long enough to get to know anyone, let alone make any enemies. Aside from the few that he mentioned—and he agreed, those motives where shaky at best—he could think of no one who might want him gone.

Mostly, he was bothered by the first part of the letter. Not only did someone want him gone, but they knew something about his father. Something Will wasn't sure he wanted to find out.

Chapter Nine

Will was glad when Caralee changed the subject. "Hey, why haven't I seen Bruno? Is he still too afraid to come out of hiding?"

"He's getting better, actually. He's over there, under the table, hiding from the scary lady who showed up with dinner."

"He's the first one to ever think I'm scary." She laughed. "I'll try not to let it go to my head."

"If it helps keep you humble, he thought the broom was absolutely terrifying when I tried to sweep up a while ago."

"I'm as intimidating as a broom? Yeah, that's humbling. So, what have you guys been up to other than finding threatening letters? The yard looks amazing."

"Thanks," he said. "I thought it might be good to work inside for a while, get him used to the house. I made a list of things that need repair, so I started on them. First up was this dripping faucet. See? No more drips."

"Wonderful! That's been bugging me for ages. Thank you so much."

"It's not overstepping if I just work on stuff?"

"Not at all," she assured him. "It's obvious you know what you're doing, so have at it. I'm all thumbs when it comes to home repairs, and Grandpa will sure appreciate getting these things done. My father was going to start on some of them when they get back in town, but that's not for a couple months."

"Your parents don't live in the area?"

"They do, but just before Grandpa went into the hospital, they left for a three-month mission trip. My dad retired last year, and this has been something they've planned for a long time."

"Good for them. It's a shame your grandfather got so sick while they've been gone."

"They offered to come back, but Grandpa won't hear of it. And my brother just started a new job in Detroit, so he doesn't have much vacation time saved up."

"So everything fell on your shoulders. I guess sometimes having family isn't really that much of an advantage, after all."

"We're here for each other when it counts. Come on, grab a plate and help yourself," she said, opening the various food containers she'd set out.

They were quiet as they each filled a plateful and found a spot to sit. He brought out the iced tea he'd made earlier, and Caralee grabbed glasses from the cupboard. Bruno panted nervously but made no effort to run to another room. It was surprisingly comfortable to be sharing a meal with Caralee in her grandfather's kitchen.

"So how was church today?" Will asked when they were seated, not sure what else to say.

"It was good," she replied. "Pastor Donaldson was preaching on one of Jesus's parables, the Prodigal Son."

"The story of a young man who takes his father's money and wastes it all on wild living until he's lost everything, right?"

"You've heard it, I guess."

"The kid hits rock bottom, ends up homeless and hungry. That's when he crawls back to his father looking for handouts."

"He goes home to his father seeking forgiveness," Caralee corrected. "The father welcomes him, gives him clean clothes and throws a big celebration. It's a reminder of God's endless love."

"Right, but don't forget there's an older brother, too."

"You *do* know the story. I thought you didn't do church stuff."

"I don't, but that doesn't mean I never did."

"So you're the modern-day prodigal son, are you?"

"Because I left the fold? Hmm, if I'm the prodigal because I left, are you the older brother because you stayed?"

"Maybe," she admitted. "Pastor Donaldson's lesson today was primarily about the prodigal and how wonderful it was for him to be welcomed home, but of course we can't forget the older brother."

Will was all too familiar with that part of the story. He understood it better than she knew.

"It's great that the prodigal got a second chance," he agreed. "But it didn't do much for the older brother, did it? He did all the right things, staying home and working hard. He served his father faithfully every single day, and now they're having this big party without him. His useless brother was getting treated like a prince."

"Yes, the older brother felt left out," she agreed. "He thought he deserved that party a lot more than his brother did."

"And you don't think he did? After all those years of working hard and doing everything he was asked to do…everything he could to make his father proud?" Will asked.

Now Caralee paused. Her forehead creased as she pondered his words. "But that's the point of the story, isn't it? The one who thinks he has earned grace really doesn't understand what grace is."

"I guess I just don't have enough grace in me to dole it out so easily for others," he said.

"Then it's a good thing you don't have to, isn't it?" she said.

"Yeah. Hey, isn't there something else we can talk about? How's your grandfather doing?"

"Sure, we can change the subject," she said, although he knew she planned to bring it back up again at some point. "Grandpa's doing pretty well, thanks. I don't see how he's getting any rest with all the visitors he has, though. Just as I was leaving, the DeBonets showed up."

"Who?"

"Frank and Geneva DeBonet. Friends from church. Actually, I talked to them after the service today, and they had some interesting information. I never realized it, but your parents' affair wasn't such a big secret, after all."

"No, it wasn't," he agreed.

This wasn't a topic he liked any better than Bible stories about good sons and bad sons, but Caralee would need to know about it. No matter whose body he'd found in the garden, any events connected to that house in the past had to be investigated. He'd have to air their dirty laundry, like it or not.

"How did your mother meet Willard Viveners?" she asked. "Did she live here in Blossom Township, or was she from somewhere else?"

"She's from Cleveland. She was in nursing school and came here to do an internship, I believe. That's how she met my father."

"I wasn't aware he worked in the medical field."

"I don't think he did, but she never talked about him much. Anyway, they had a fling, and she went back to Cleveland to finish school. I guess they kept seeing each other, because a year later, I came along and he promised to marry her. We all know how that turned out."

"Yes, either he chose *not* to marry her, or…"

"Or he died. Either way, not a very happy ending."

"No, it's not," Caralee said with a sigh. "So your mother raised you on her own?"

"Yep. Her family had no interest in me or in their black sheep of a daughter. When it was obvious my father wasn't in the picture, she took a job in Pennsylvania and never looked back."

"And it was just the two of you all your life."

"Well…most of my life," he replied, taking a deep breath before continuing. "I do have a stepfather."

Caralee couldn't help but wonder why Will hadn't mentioned a stepfather before now. Everything about his demeanor told her that whoever this stepfather was, he was not someone Will wanted to discuss. But Cara-lee needed to know.

"Your mother married?" she asked gently.

"During my last year of high school," he answered. "They met at church, and he swept her off her feet. I was so happy for her, finding the right guy after all that time."

"So you didn't mind having a stepfather?"

"No, I was thrilled, to be honest. He seemed perfect for us. He made her happy, and he was the father figure I never had. He got us a nice house, new cars, and brought me into his real estate business."

"That's how you learned to do renovations."

"Yeah. He sent me on jobs with his crews. It was great. I thought *he* was great. He went to church with us, mentored me and gave us all a bright future. While my friends struggled to pay for college, I was flipping houses with him. I made six figures a year by the time I was twenty-one. Everything seemed perfect until…"

"Until?"

"Until I found out what he really was. But by then, it was too late. I was up to my eyebrows in his dirty deals. It was just a matter of time before it all came crashing down around us, and it did."

"Oh no! He was a crook? What happened?"

"I went to prison, and he escaped to some tropical island that doesn't extradite."

"But…your mother?"

"Abandoned again. She still won't believe what he did. He took everything they had when he left, and somehow she blames me for it all."

"Blames you? But how can she—"

"Don't ask. It's not something I want to talk about, okay?"

"Okay, sure…but no wonder you have trust issues."

"That's an understatement. But seriously, whining about my troubles won't help figure out the mystery of that body I found. Did you talk to anyone else at your church? Any more old-timers who might remember something from the past?"

Will clearly didn't want to share more from his painful past, so she was happy to return to the case. "Actually, I did! Not at church, but my grandfather had a pretty dramatic story for me. He told me something that happened in Blossom Township about twenty-nine years ago."

"Coincidentally, I was born twenty-nine years ago."

"I know. I looked it up. You were probably a few months old at the time. We know for a fact your father was still living here then."

"My mother was in Cleveland with me, waiting for him to get his divorce. Instead, he was still living with Violet?"

"All I know is he had a pest control business here in Blossom Township. One night, the place burned to the ground. My grandfather suspected arson, but he could never prove anything. Your father and his business partner turned in a nice hefty claim to their insurance company. Not only did the building burn, but there was over half a million dollars in cash in their office at the time."

"Whoa! What were they doing with that kind of cash? No one keeps that much money sitting around in their office."

"Right? My grandfather thought the whole thing felt

shady. There were rumors that the money never even existed, or maybe it did but didn't actually burn. Grandpa thought one of the partners may have taken it and then set the fire to hide their theft."

"Not a bad con, if they could get away with it. Pocket the money, then get it back from the insurance, too."

"Well, they didn't get it back. The insurance company questioned the claim and wouldn't pay out. When your father disappeared shortly after that, it seemed like proof of guilt to everyone. They assumed he stole the cash, burned the business and left his partner in the lurch."

"Sounds familiar, poor guy. Whatever happened to him?"

"I just saw him and his wife in church this morning. Frank and Geneva DeBonet."

"Small world," he said. Then she watched his expression go cloudy again. "This only gets worse and worse for me, doesn't it? First I think my father abandoned me, then I wonder if he was murdered, then you suggest maybe he committed the murder, and now I might have to get used to knowing he stole from his partner and was an arsonist. What other wonderful things am I going to learn about him?"

"I don't know. Are you still willing to supply that DNA sample you suggested?"

"More than ever. I need answers, Caralee. Even if I won't like them."

"Even if those answers are dangerous?" she asked. "That letter isn't a joke, Will. Someone knows what went on back then, and they seem to want to get rid of you."

"I'm not going anywhere," he assured her. "I can't. My truck's still in impound, remember?"

"We'll get it back for you tomorrow," she promised.

"Great, but I'm still not leaving. Did you learn anything else about the arson case?"

"Only that the insurance investigator came to Blossom Township and never left."

"The guy investigating the fire? Was he murdered here, too?"

"Nope, married. And you've met him—D.R. Fields."

"The slick real estate guy? Your old boyfriend's dad?"

"Tad Fields was *not* my boyfriend," she reminded him yet again. "But yeah, that's the guy. While he was here to investigate, I guess he met Tad's mom and they ended up getting married. When the case was closed, D.R. stayed here. He quit working for the insurance company and went into real estate."

"But he knows some things about my father."

"He might. Are you sure you want to know anything more?"

Will seemed to consider this for a moment. A long moment. She could tell he wasn't sure, not really. Maybe it was true that he wasn't afraid of that letter, but clearly the unknown truth loomed much more frightening. She couldn't imagine how hard it must be to wonder all your life who your father was, then suddenly face the possibility that he could have been a monster.

"Yeah," Will replied finally. "I need to know."

Chapter Ten

Monday morning had arrived bright and early. Cara-lee was still contemplating all the things she and Will had discussed yesterday. Mostly, she was surprised by how much she was contemplating Will.

How had this kind, decent man been forced to pay for his stepfather's crimes? She'd stayed up late, finding the court documents and reading through them online. The Will she was coming to know couldn't have done what he was accused of—cheating hardworking families out of their homes, conning a dozen elderly people into losing their life savings, endangering lives by using shoddy building materials and falsifying inspection documentation.

And yet, he'd offered no proof that he hadn't done those things. He'd been found guilty, paid huge fines and served four years in prison. Why would he have not provided a better defense? Something just didn't add up. He was quite a puzzle, if she could only put the pieces together.

"How long do you think those DNA results will take?" Will asked as he strolled into her office.

"You're done with the CSI people? They got the samples they needed?"

"Yep. Just an easy cheek swab. They seem like good people, but I much prefer the personnel in this office." He grinned. She felt her cheeks growing warm.

"I'm surprised you're willing to step foot in here."

"It's not so bad as long as I know I'll be leaving again, and that your Sergeant Billings is still posted on night duty."

"He won't be giving you any more trouble. And everything is sorted out with your truck?"

"It is. Thanks for waiving the fees on that impound. I really appreciate it."

"You're welcome," she said, happy to have helped him. "No charges were filed, so you don't owe us anything. I'm just sorry for how it all worked out. No hard feelings?"

"You're a good cop, Caralee," he said. "I appreciate what you've done for me. I know I wasn't making your life easy that first night, that's for sure. You didn't get mad, though, and you defused a bad situation before it got worse. You treated me better than I deserved, so no, there are no hard feelings."

"Good, because I was just about to ask you to help me."

"Oh, yeah?" He stepped farther into her office, leaning in to see what she'd been working on with the pile of files stacked on her desk.

"I'm happy to say that we won't have to wait long for your DNA results," she announced. "Since we're just matching yours to the samples from the body, we don't have to run it through the state database. They should be able to process your sample within forty-eight hours."

"Wow, that's pretty quick. I'm not sure I'm ready to find out so soon."

"Of course you are," she assured him. "But while we wait, I thought you could help look at my grandfather's old case files from that fire at your father's business almost thirty years ago. Another pair of eyes is always appreciated, and since you're already involved in this case…"

He smiled and finished her sentence. "You might as well put me to work. Good idea. I guess even if it turns out not to be my father's body, whoever ended up buried there could have had something to do with the suspicious fire."

"Right. So I'm trying to compile a list of everyone who was involved, anyone who would've had something to lose or gain from the fire and possible insurance fraud afterward."

"What have you found so far?"

She was happy that he was so interested in helping. Usually when she was faced with a dilemma, she'd go to her parents or even her brother, but they weren't around right now. And she refused to put more of a burden on Grandpa. He had looked so tired the last time she saw him. Right now, she needed someone who could offer a second point of view as she pored over these files, someone familiar with this case and invested in it. Right now, she needed Will.

"I haven't found much more than we already knew," she said. "Your father was business partners with Frank

DeBonet. They were in pest control and had plans to expand the business, add on to their building and get new equipment…that sort of thing."

"Which is why they had all that cash on hand…or so they said."

"Right. Apparently Frank claimed half of the money he put in was his, and the rest was your father's. When the place burned, all the money was lost."

"Unless it wasn't," Will added.

"Exactly. My grandfather was investigating the fire. He and the fire marshal at the time thought there was a good possibility it was arson. They notified the insurance company of their concerns."

"And the company sent D.R. Fields here to investigate," Will said. "I get the idea he suspected more than just arson."

"Yeah. Grandpa has a copy of the reports D.R. sent to his firm. It indicates that he looked at bank records for both men and couldn't find any record of the so-called missing money."

"That's very interesting," Will acknowledged, craning his neck to see the file.

Caralee pushed it closer for him to see. He pulled up a chair and sat down across from her, his eyes glued to the file. She could only imagine what it must feel like to be learning things about your parent for the first time—things that might not be so good.

"So, naturally D.R. advises his company not to pay out. If the money really didn't exist, the men were trying to commit fraud. But look here," she said, reaching to turn the page for him.

Her hand unexpectedly brushed his. It was just the

slightest touch and shouldn't have meant anything at all. Ordinarily, she wouldn't have even noticed. But Will was hardly ordinary.

Her glance shot up to meet his. He smiled, then just simply turned back to the pages. Her cheeks were heating up again, and she was glad he'd looked away. They were working here, nothing more. She did *not* want Will to get the wrong idea. She herself didn't want to have any ideas at all, at least not about Will and his unsettling smile.

"All of a sudden, D.R. turned in this report," she said, eager to bring the focus back to their work. "His final determination was that the money *did* exist, and your father probably stole it."

"Kind of a huge leap from the first report, isn't it?" Will asked.

"Yes, and I can't find anything that mentions how he got to that conclusion. I see his notes here for his investigation, then suddenly, no more notes—they just aren't here."

"That's very interesting. Up to that point, it looks like he kept a lot of notes. I wonder what he learned that made him change his mind so drastically?"

"I don't know," Caralee said with a sigh. "But it sure does give Frank DeBonet plenty of motive to be upset with your father."

"That would put Frank on the top of our suspect list. If the money did exist, and if it didn't burn in the fire, Frank had the most to gain from keeping it secret. If my father stole the money and set the fire, Frank could have murdered him out of anger and taken the money back. Then again, if the money didn't exist, Frank could have covered that fact by killing my father to make it seem like he'd taken the money and run off with it. Frank could have gotten away with arson and murder, even if he didn't get the insurance payout."

"Obviously, I'll need to talk to Frank again," Caralee said.

She pulled out a notepad and wrote Frank's name at the top. She didn't stop there, though. As she'd been looking at the old case files, she'd come across a few other things. Frank wasn't the only one with something to gain.

"But then there's this. Read this interview that Jewel gave when my grandfather talked to her about the fire."

Will frowned in confusion, taking the next folder she handed him. "Jewel? What does my nosy neighbor have to do with that fire?"

"Nothing, but my grandfather thought she might have seen or heard something, being next door to his home. Look what she says about that."

He read a few lines, then his eyes went wide. "She says she hardly knew Violet or my father! You told me she was longtime best buds with Violet, and she used to come over while you were visiting."

"Right? I suppose it could be true that she didn't know them very well back then, but I looked it up. Jewel lived there several years before the fire. She had plenty of time to get to know her neighbors. Her answer to my grandfather seems like...like she's hiding something."

"You think she knew about the arson? That my father had stolen or lied about that money?"

"Or maybe she just didn't want to get involved. Either way, I clearly need to talk to her and find out more about what was going on back then, and why she's so secretive now."

"Keeping to your house and not wanting to tattle on your neighbors doesn't necessarily mean you're guilty of murder," Will noted.

"But it could mean you're hiding something. I'm putting her on the list."

"Okay. But she's not the only one. What about that inspector? He should definitely be on the list."

"D.R. Fields? I suppose we can add him, but why?"

"He changed his mind too quickly."

She laughed. "If that's a crime, we're all in trouble."

"Come on, doesn't it seem…out of character? He's the kind of guy who thinks he knows everything, that he's right all the time. He wouldn't just change his mind for no reason."

"Maybe he found some evidence."

"Why didn't he list it in the report? And honestly, quitting his job and suddenly having the capital to launch a whole new career is kind of suspicious. And why did he show up at my house a couple days ago asking all those questions?"

"You're right, it's suspicious. I'll put him on the list."

"So we've got Frank, Jewel, and now D.R. I guess we need to consider Violet, too," Will said, cocking his mouth to one side as he thought about it. "I know she's gone now, but she had the best access to the site and, if my father is the victim, she certainly had motive."

"True, but then we can't overlook his mistress. She couldn't have been very happy about all the time he was spending here instead of with *her*."

"You're saying my *mother* is a suspect?"

She realized what she'd said. Somehow she'd gotten so wrapped up in this riddle, thinking through who was involved and what motive they might have had, that she completely forgot this was Will's actual life they were talking about. She wanted to crawl under her desk.

"I'm sorry, Will. I'm just thinking out loud. Of course there's no reason to suspect your mother. She's not mentioned at all in these files, and there's no evidence she was ever in Blossom Township at that time."

"No, I understand. You have to consider all the possibilities. But I was going to call my mother today, let her know what's happening. Is that a conflict of interest? Maybe I shouldn't be here."

Caralee realized he was right. Whether or not his mother was a suspect, she certainly was a person of interest. Caralee should have thought of that before now.

"You haven't told your mother about this yet?" she asked.

He shook his head. "We're not on the best of terms these days, I'm sorry to say."

"That's too bad. I'm going to have to talk to her about this at some point. Are you okay with that?"

"Yeah. I'll give you her phone number."

"You should talk to her, too, Will. She's your mother. Call her later, okay?"

"Yeah, sure. Later."

Caralee didn't know what else to say. It was pretty clear Will didn't want to talk about it, and she could understand. He said his mother blamed him for what his stepfather had done. She couldn't imagine how painful that must be for him.

She cleared her throat and turned her attention back to their work.

"So we've got three suspects and one person of interest. First, I'll focus on the one suspect who had the most at stake."

"Frank?"

"Right. You've got your truck now, so you're free to come and go as you please. You might as well go back to Grandpa's and check on Bruno. Then really, Will, call your mother. She should probably know what's going on."

"After all this time…it'll be a lot to process. You sure you don't need me to do anything else?"

"One more thing. I know you aren't taking that letter you got very seriously, but we still don't know who that came from, or why. Be careful, Will."

"I'll be fine." He smiled at her again. "I've got Bruno to protect me."

Will sat in his truck and blew out a frustrated breath. He'd gone home and walked Bruno, then found some cobwebs in the garage to sweep out, and finally tried to call his mother. She didn't answer. He wondered if Caralee had reached her already.

Was his mother honestly busy with something, or was she just avoiding him? They hadn't spoken since he told her he was coming here to fix up this old house. She hadn't wanted him to come, hadn't wanted him to have anything to do with this house or Blossom Township. He'd told her she was being melodramatic, and he'd left.

Now he wished he'd done more to heal the rift between them. He missed her. He hoped she was okay.

It was frustrating to just sit around, feeling useless. Wasn't there anything more he could be doing to solve this case?

Caralee had said she was going to talk to Frank DeBonet, but he wasn't the only one on that list of suspects. Maybe Will could pay a visit to the nearby real estate office of their good friend D.R. Fields. He had told Will to call on him anytime and talk about selling his house, hadn't he?

Well, this seemed like the perfect time.

Will drove the couple blocks to D.R.'s office and parked on the street. A big red awning hung over the door with a bright sign announcing the owner's name. D.R. had named his company after himself, of course. It looked like he occupied quite a lot of space in the building, too.

"I see you've finally come to your senses and dropped in to talk about making some money," D.R. said when Will entered.

He got the feeling the man must've been stalking the window of his office and then come pouncing out into the reception area the minute a potential customer showed up. D.R. hadn't even let the young woman at the front desk offer a greeting before he swooped in on Will. She just rolled her eyes and went back to doodling on a sketch pad. Apparently business here wasn't quite as brisk as D.R. would have everyone believe.

D.R. draped an arm over Will's shoulders to lead him into his office, which was a stark contrast to the more than hundred-year-old building it was in. From the outside, D.R. Fields Real Estate & Property Management appeared to be a standard small-town business on the ground floor of a nineteenth-century, three-story building. The huge front windows had probably once displayed feed supplies, mercantile items or perhaps knickknacks from a long-gone five-and-dime.

Today D.R.'s office looked more like a spaceship. His furniture was ultramodern, gleaming with glass and gold-colored metal. Will supposed the place was meant to engender awe and a view toward a bright future, although he couldn't help but think it out of place and too pretentious for Blossom Township.

And Will certainly knew about pretentions. He'd worked for his stepfather for ten years, after all. When it came to schmoozing and showy ostentation, D.R. Fields had nothing on James Riordan. For too long, Will had tried to be just like him.

"So, are you ready to get this ball rolling?" D.R. said, dropping into his throne-like desk chair. "I can promise you top dollar for your place. We can get this wrapped up in two weeks, tops."

"Two weeks? That's pretty quick."

"I don't let grass grow under my feet. I've been watching you, Will, and I see someone who's ready to move on. Believe it or not, I've already got a buyer for you."

"Already? I'm not even your client."

"Details! Now, let's just say they've got the financing all worked out. This can be a cash transaction! How does that sound to you?"

It sounded like he ought to get up and run away from this place, that was how it sounded. Even his rotten stepfather had at least tried to seem a little less shady. Did D.R. really think he'd fall for this pie-in-the-sky kind of thing? Obviously, he did.

Will decided to play along.

"Wow, that's almost too good to be true! As you can probably guess, I've been short on cash these days. A quick sale sure would help out."

D.R. smiled, the snake oil practically oozing from his pores. "Of course it would. And I can make it happen for you. I mean, we've got to wait on that silly investigation, but I'm sure they'll be done in a couple days. The guy's been dead thirty years, after all. How many clues do they think they're still going to find over there?"

"So you're pretty sure you know who that body belongs to," Will stated. "Maybe you know something the police investigators don't?"

"Come on, I hate to be insensitive, but we both know there's only one scenario that makes any sense. Sorry for your loss, but it's obvious that body has to be Willard Viveners, Sr."

"The police have released a statement?"

"They don't have to! We all know. Maybe you haven't heard, but I was an investigator back then," D.R. said, propping his elbows on the table and leaning in, as if to share some great wisdom. "For an insurance company. Your father, I'm sad to say, wasn't a nice man. He committed insurance fraud and stole from his business partner."

"I heard that case was never really settled."

"He settled it when he took off! That was proof enough for all of us that he was guilty."

"But if he took off, why are you so certain that's his body out there?"

D.R. stared silently at Will. "Um, I mean…we all *as-*

sumed he'd taken off. When you found that body out there, it was obvious he hadn't."

"So the case wasn't settled. You simply used his disappearance as a convenient reason to stop investigating."

"There just didn't seem to be any point continuing once he wasn't around," D.R. said, as if that were a logical explanation for letting someone get away with a crime.

"You claimed he had run off, you quit your job and started up your own business. Good thing you had enough capital to do that. How much did it cost to start up your own brokerage back then? It couldn't have been cheap."

"My wife's family helped us," he said quickly. "And I don't think I like what you're implying."

"I'm just curious how you're so sure that my father has been dead all this time when your investigation apparently proved he was alive. And why are you so eager to get me out of that house, out of Blossom Township?"

"I'm not! I'm just... I'm trying to help you. You want to sell the place, don't you?"

D.R. was practically sweating now. Will realized he'd hit a nerve. Could he have found his mystery mailman? D.R. was so eager to get his hands on Will's house it was entirely possible he'd sent that threatening letter to scare him away.

"Where were you on Sunday afternoon?" Will asked.

D.R. blinked. "Um, I was home. My son Tad is coming back to town later today, and I was getting the spare room fixed up for him. You can ask my wife. After church, we stopped for lunch, then were at home moving furniture all day."

"All day? Didn't have to run out to pick up dinner, or anything?"

"No, we ate in. And what's this about?" D.R. growled. "I don't appreciate being questioned. I told your police chief Tad was coming home—they used to be an item. Now that he's spent the last years making it big in the financial markets, I'm sure she can hardly wait to cozy up to him again."

"She mentioned they used to be friends."

"Yeah, they did. Did she mention they were homecoming king and queen? Local people tend to stick together around here. I've told you all I know about that body you found, and I'm sorry if you don't want to believe it's probably your dad. Now, if you're not really here to talk business, then I've got things I need to do. Time is money, and you've been wasting mine."

Will recognized a dismissal when he heard one. If D.R. did know anything more—and Will was pretty sure he did—he wasn't about to tell him now. All he'd managed to do was tip him off that his history as an investigator was being considered. Will hoped this didn't cause problems for Caralee. She'd want to talk to D.R. at some point, and it was highly unlikely the man would be forthcoming with her after this.

Sadly, the only new thing Will had learned from this conversation was that he truly disliked Tad Fields, and he hadn't even met him. Yet.

Chapter Eleven

Caralee pulled up in front of the DeBonets' manicured home. As expected, flowers were blooming in the landscaping, and everything showed immaculate care and attention to detail. It was a known fact that people drove down Beechridge Street just to get a look at the house with all its beautiful gardening.

Caralee's reason today was a bit more educational. At least, she hoped it would be. She didn't want the DeBonets to feel like they were being interrogated.

"Look who's here!" Frank called from the flower bed at the front corner of the house.

He was wearing a canvas hat and muddy work gloves. The wheelbarrow and tools scattered around him suggested he'd been eradicating any foolish weed that might have dared to sprout in his garden. He pulled off his gloves and waved at her, calling over his shoulder to Geneva, who must have been working in the back.

"Hey, our favorite little police chief is here!"

She inwardly cringed at the condescending greeting. It was insulting—unintentionally, she hoped—but still she bristled. How was she ever going to feel like a competent chief when everyone in town kept reminding her she was not?

Geneva came around the side of the house, wiping her hands on a many-pocketed smock. At church it had almost seemed as if Geneva regretted Frank inviting her over, but today she appeared happy for the visit. Caralee returned her smile.

"I'm so glad you stopped by," Geneva said as she approached. "Come around to the back. I was just going to stop for some lemonade. That's the beauty of being retired. We can work when we want or take an early lunch break."

Caralee remarked on the beautiful plantings as she followed the DeBonets into their backyard. The patio umbrella was raised, putting a table with four chairs into welcome shade. A pitcher of lemonade was set out with a few glasses. Butterflies fluttered among the many pots of showy annuals.

"Everything is doing so well for you," Caralee said, stooping to smell a brilliantly red rose climbing high on a trellis.

"We're hoping for good things at the flower show this year," Geneva said. "Frank's been urging his dahlias along, and I've got a new daylily I'm ready to introduce. It's an early bloomer."

"Oh! How wonderful. I'm sure that'll be very exciting for everyone."

"Well, not for anyone else who hopes to take the prize in that category." Geneva laughed, although Caralee knew she was only half kidding. These people were serious about winning.

"I guess I missed seeing all your tulips in bloom," Caralee said, noting the area where the foliage remained without any blooms.

"Yes, we'll be cutting those down soon. They were gorgeous this year, I'll say that. But see the irises? They're blooming like crazy for me."

Caralee did indeed see the irises. There was a whole area devoted just to them, all different colors. She walked over to get a closer look, strolling along the contoured bed, finding herself surrounded by huge blooms in yellow, pink, white and purple. Some of them had multiple colors and intricate patterns showing on the petals. The collection they had here was quite impressive.

"These are really stunning," Caralee commented. "And that's your daylily bed over there?"

"Yes, we've still got a couple weeks before they're blooming in earnest."

"It looks like something has started early," Caralee said, moving toward the flash of red and gold that caught her eye.

The daylily bed was a large area, roughly oval-shaped, with probably thirty or forty different plants growing in green, spiky clumps. Several of them had tall scapes with buds forming on them, but one was already fully open today. Caralee gazed in amazement.

The colors were so vibrant! The bloom was large, the main body of it almost neon red, but the edges had flaming gold ruffles that sparkled in the sunlight. In the center of the bloom, the throat was deep gold and radiated like a star out onto the petals. It was a very striking bloom, and extra special because it was blooming earlier than the others.

Even more than all that, Caralee found herself speechless at the sight. Not only was it beautiful, but it was familiar. She knew this bloom—she'd seen it before, six years ago in, Violet Viveners's garden.

At that time, Violet had been just getting ready to introduce it. She'd told Caralee she'd hybridized the flower herself and had been keeping it a secret. She was going to register it and show it for the first time at the flower show that year. She'd worked hard to selectively grow something that would bloom just in time for that annual event. And she'd given it a name.

She'd called it *Miss Caralee.*

"It's…very pretty," she managed to say. "What is it called?"

"I'm calling it *DeBonets' Dancer.* We're planning to register it and everything. Frank says he's talked to a wholesaler who might be interested in marketing it. Wouldn't that be wonderful?"

"Yes, yes it would."

"We're very proud of this."

"I can certainly understand that. Is this a hybrid that you created yourselves?"

"Yes! Frank's been helping me cross-pollinate our daylilies for several years now. We keep a seedling bed behind the greenhouse and most of them aren't very special, sadly. This one, as you can see, is definitely a keeper! Frank found it growing back there and brought it up to this bed a couple years ago so we could monitor it. Now I'm finally ready for everyone to see it."

"Great, but I…well, didn't I see one like it at Violet's house some years ago?"

Geneva shook her head with certainty. "No, she never

had one like this. I helped care for her garden after she passed, you may recall. I would know if she had one like this."

"Hmm, yes, you probably would."

Caralee was careful not to say any more. What if she was wrong? She wasn't a daylily expert, after all. Still, Violet had been so proud of her flower and had named it after Caralee, so she had a very clear mental image of the flower.

So who had created it? It seemed too much of a coincidence that they had both grown such similar flowers. Not only was the color and pattern of the bloom the same as the one in Caralee's memory, but it was the same height, and Violet's lily had also bloomed a couple weeks earlier than the others. It just couldn't be a different plant!

Geneva must have taken it for herself. Violet had kept it secret, so perhaps Geneva had no idea anyone else had seen it. The whole town was aware that Violet kept her garden off-limits to nearly everyone. Perhaps Geneva saw it blooming while she was caring for the garden and decided she wanted to take credit for it. She could have dug the plant and put it in with her own seedlings, letting it grow and mature right along with them.

And there was nothing Caralee could do about it. If she said anything, it would be her uncertain word against the DeBonets'. Who would believe her? She wasn't even sure she believed herself.

Perhaps "Miss Caralee," the flower Violet had named for her, was just a faded memory and had been truly lost.

"I'm sure it will be a big hit at the flower show," she said finally.

"That's what we're hoping for!" Geneva beamed as Frank approached them. "Come, take a seat. I need to get off my feet for a bit."

She joined them at the patio table. The lemonade was very refreshing. If not for the way her brain kept chewing on questions and clues regarding everything that had been going on, Caralee would have found sitting here among the flowers and shrubbery of the DeBonets' yard very relaxing.

"So, what really brought you over here?" Frank asked. "I'm glad you enjoy the flowers, but I think you've got something on your mind."

Caralee chuckled at his candor. "Yes, I came by with a few questions that might help me with the case. Is that all right? Do you mind giving me a couple more minutes?"

"I don't know what we could possibly have to tell you that you don't already know," Geneva said. "Hasn't the sheriff been able to help at all?"

"He's assisting, yes, but this is my case. Since we all know Mr. Viveners lived in that house before he went missing, I need to gather information about him during that time."

"So you want to know about the fire," Frank added. "Everyone had a lot of questions about that back then. I imagine your grandfather has a whole big file about it."

"He does," she said. "I've looked through it. You were very helpful at the time, giving interviews and providing documentation and copies of the insurance reports."

"You know they never did pay out on that?" he said. "I was sore over that for a long time."

"We nearly lost our home!" Geneva added. "All his hard work, everything we had was sunk into that business, and then…well, you know what happened."

"There was a fire," Caralee said. "Your business was a total loss."

Frank sighed. "It was awful. And you know about that money, too, don't you? All my life savings, gone… just like that."

"Well, that's what I'd like to talk about. Your claim to the insurance company states that an unusually large amount of cash was being kept in the office, in a desk."

"It was around half a million," Frank said. "We didn't usually keep that much on hand, of course, but Willard came into some money, so I said that I would match his amount and we would expand our business. I should've known something wasn't quite right when he insisted I bring my money in cash."

"That does seem kind of questionable," Caralee agreed.

"He was my partner, and I trusted him," Frank said, gulping down the rest of his lemonade. "Even after the fire, I believed he'd left the money there, that it had burned."

"What was it specifically that the insurance company began to question?" Caralee asked.

"What *didn't* they question?" Frank grumbled with a roll of his eyes. "But that's their job, I suppose. They sent a real eager beaver. Did you know that was D.R. Fields? He came here as their investigator."

"Yes, I was surprised to see that in the files. Did he first raise the suspicions?"

"I think so. He came in with a chip on his shoulder,

though, convinced they weren't going to pay out on our claim, and he was going to prove we were scamming them."

"That seems pretty rude," Caralee noted. "I guess he wasn't your favorite person for a while. How did you let go of that when he stayed here?"

"Well, he's still not my favorite person, but I can't hold it against him after all this time. What's done is done. He had his suspicions and, well, it turns out he was right."

"So you came to believe that Willard actually stole the money and set the fire to cover it up?"

"I didn't want to believe it, but yeah. Once he took off when D.R. started poking into things, I had to face the facts."

"What was D.R. poking into that made him so nervous?"

"Bank statements. They wanted to find proof that we really did have that kind of money. My share of the money came from a family trust. I never did find out where his came from—if his share ever existed."

"You think he'd lied about putting his share of the money in?"

"I don't know where he would have got it. Money was one thing he and Violet fought over all the time. It seemed like he never had enough for her. Anything he'd get, she'd take it and put it right into the house."

"So when they started looking at his bank accounts, they saw he never had money saved up, and he couldn't have put in his share like he said he did."

"Exactly," Geneva said. "Why else would he be so desperate to get out of town before they found out? He knew they were just about to prove he was a crook. He took our money and left!"

Frank sounded less convinced. "Then again, if that was him buried out there… I guess he *didn't* get out of town."

"Someone must've been angry enough or desperate enough to kill him," Caralee said. "If that *was* him out there, of course."

"Well, I didn't do it!" Frank insisted. "I was mad at him, sure. I hated him for a good long time. But I never killed him."

"You're saying you just got over it."

"What else could I do? He was gone, and so was my business and my money. I figured he got away with it and was living the high life somewhere with his mistress."

"And you never tried to find him?"

"Of course I did! I begged D.R. to give me his reports, to let me know anything that might help me figure out where Willard had gone. He wouldn't, though. He said that was privileged information and belonged to the insurance company."

"But they closed the case."

"Yeah, Willard left, so they declared insurance fraud and refused to pay. My old partner got away with half a million dollars!"

Caralee hated to point out the obvious, but it needed to be said.

"Or maybe he didn't. Maybe someone got away with murder."

Caralee left the DeBonets' house feeling like she had more questions now than when she'd arrived. The whole idea of keeping five hundred thousand dollars was hard to swallow, but Frank seemed to have honestly believed it was there. And what was she to think of Geneva claiming Violet's daylily as her own?

So far, her prayers for wisdom and guidance seemed to have been going unanswered. How would she solve this crime if she couldn't tie all these threads together? It looked like Willard had lied about things, but now so had Geneva. Did Caralee really have any reason to trust that Frank was telling the truth?

She needed to find Will. He'd want to know how her phone call with his mother had gone, and he'd surely have ideas about what she'd learned from Frank and Geneva. Maybe she'd run over to the house to see him. They were good when they brainstormed together; he could help her make sense of some of it, if there was any sense to it at all.

The noonday sun was hot now, and she was glad for the shade of Grandpa's big sycamore tree when she pulled into his driveway. She hopped out and heard her name being called. A quick glance brought a wide smile to her face.

Grandpa's neighbor, Mr. Jackson, was walking his dog on the sidewalk. He paused to chat with Caralee, asking after her grandfather and assuring her that his whole family had been keeping him in their prayers. She really appreciated that.

"Oh, and I'm sure you're happy to have Tad Fields back in town for a while," Mr. Jackson said with a sly grin.

"Yes, I heard he'll be back soon," she said, not bothering to correct the man's obvious impression that she might have some special interest in Tad's whereabouts.

"Oh, he's back already," Mr. Jackson informed her. "I saw him a couple days ago, coming out of the courthouse."

"Probably helping his dad with some real estate stuff," she said. "I'm sure D.R. is happy to have him back."

"And I'll bet he's not the only one." He chuckled, then had to steady himself as his rambunctious dog tried to continue their walk. "All right, Bucky, we'll keep going. It's good to see you, Caralee! Give your grandfather hugs from all of us."

She assured him she would. Once again, she was very thankful for good friends and good neighbors. Without them, how would she get through?

She headed up to the house and knocked. Bruno barked inside, and she couldn't help but smile. It was good hearing a dog in the house again; it made it feel more like home. And she was glad the puppy was feeling secure enough to actually bark at things, instead of just hide from them.

Will answered the door. She was even more happy to see him than she realized. He smiled, then noticed Mr. Jackson going by.

"That's my goal. I'm going to get Bruno to walk like that, head up, tail wagging and happy to be out there."

"That's a good goal. Mr. Jackson and Bucky might be able to give you some pointers. He's a nice guy. Lives just over there," she said, pointing at the man's house.

"Ah, I thought I heard voices out here. You were catching up with him?"

"Only briefly. He seemed to think I'd be interested to know about Tad Fields coming back to town."

Will nodded, ushering her inside. "Yeah, D.R. is all excited. I guess he comes home today?"

"Today? No, he's been here a couple days already. Wait…you talked to D.R.?"

"Um, yeah. I went over there and…a couple days? No, that can't be right. I wondered if D.R. sent me that threatening letter, so I asked him what he was doing on Sunday. He told me he was home with his wife, moving furniture and getting ready for their son, who'd be coming home later today."

Caralee frowned. "Well, that can't be right. Mr. Jackson said he saw Tad in town a couple days ago."

"So why would D.R. tell me he was still getting ready for him?"

"Because D.R. has something to hide, obviously."

Chapter Twelve

"It would make sense that D.R. could be the one who sent me that letter," Will suggested. "He was all ready to make a deal with me to get me out of the house. He sure wants me gone."

"Back up. You went to talk to him? When was this?" Caralee asked.

Will was hoping she might have skipped that question. "Um, just a little while ago. I stopped by his office."

"I thought you were coming back here to call your mother?"

"I tried to call, but she didn't answer. Did you get ahold of her?"

"I did, but don't change the subject. Why did you talk to D.R.?"

"I thought it might be helpful. He invited me to stop in anytime."

"But you shouldn't be talking about the investigation with other people."

"I wasn't! Not really. He brought it up. He seemed to think there could be no question that the body is my father's. So I asked him what he knew that the police didn't."

"And how did he react to that?"

"He used it as an opportunity to brag about how he used to be the insurance investigator on that arson case. Said he knew right from the start that there was fraud involved, and patted himself on the back for figuring out that my father obviously stole the money and ran off with it. Of course I asked him how that could be the case if he's so sure now that my father's been dead and buried all this time."

"Will, you can't be giving out information about the case!"

"I just asked him to explain how both things could be true. He basically confirmed that his only evidence against my father to begin with was that he ran away. Now that a body has been found, he's ready to admit maybe my father didn't run away."

"But why is he so interested in the house?"

"He never got around to answering that. Once I asked where he was on Sunday, he gave me that excuse about getting ready for his son to come home, then he got angry that I was questioning him and told me to leave."

"So you didn't really learn anything." Caralee sighed.

"But I did! I learned that he's pretty sure the body belongs to my father. Could it be he's really known that all along? Letting people believe my father stole money and ran away would be a great way to cover his disappearance. And now we caught him lying about his alibi for Sunday! I'm thinking you might want to talk to this guy some more."

"He's going to have his guard up now that you started

questioning him, isn't he? I'm sorry, Will, but you shouldn't have gone there."

"I got valuable information and another suspect for us."

"D.R. was already on our list."

"I don't mean him. I mean Tad."

"Tad?!"

"Yeah, just how close is he to his father? If D.R. doesn't want us to know he's been in town all weekend—despite how eager he is to get the two of you back together—maybe Tad's more involved in things than we think?"

"No, that's ridiculous. Tad's a good guy, I've known him since grade school and he's nothing like his father. I mean, he's a natural-born salesman, but he wouldn't get involved in covering up a murder."

"He might help his dad deliver a threatening letter. Whoever dropped it off certainly made a quick escape. How athletic is this guy?"

"He ran track…but seriously, he's not the threatening type. He was a bookworm, and his favorite subject in school was always art class."

"He's an artist?"

"Pretty good, too. We all loved to have him draw stuff for us, and he could do really amazing calligraphy work."

"You mean, all that fancy writing and printing, like on invitations and stuff?"

"Right. He had a real knack for that."

"So he could have done that script on the letter I got, couldn't he? He could have drafted it and written it out for his father, then delivered it and sprinted away without being seen."

"That's kind of a stretch," she said.

Will could see in her eyes that she didn't totally dismiss his words, though. He was beginning to know her pretty well. She might be defending her old school chum, but she was a cop and she wanted the truth. The clues were there and she could not overlook them, even if they added up to nothing.

Her radio crackled and dispatch interrupted their conversation. She stepped slightly away from Will to respond. The voice on the other end announced that she was needed—there was a disturbance at Will's address. Someone was harassing the investigators and preventing them from doing their job.

"I've got to go," Caralee said.

"I'm going with you," he said. "It's my house, all my things are there, and if someone is making trouble, I want to be there to know what's going on."

She seemed ready to say no, but then she simply sighed and shook her head. Apparently she was beginning to get to know him, too.

"Fine, I can't keep you away. It's your house. But respect the police line there and don't interrupt. Let us do our jobs, Will. We want to end this as much as you do."

He nodded. She was right, of course. If he went barging in over there, that wouldn't help anyone. The investigators needed to do their job, and if there was some sort of disturbance, he could trust Caralee to handle it. She'd look after his home.

"I promise," he said.

Caralee arrived at the crime scene just a minute before Will's truck pulled in behind her. She could see a couple deputies standing outside. Cars and vans lined the street, and the police tape had been removed over the front door and the iron gate to the backyard. Obviously work had been underway to process the entire scene. What was this disturbance that had called her out here?

Will trotted behind her as she went up to one of the deputies. She could hear raised voices behind the house. People inside the walled garden were having quite an argument.

"She's back there," the deputy said, directing Caralee toward the gate. "Someone said she'd probably listen to you—you'd better go on out there."

Will silently followed. They went into the cluttered backyard. Investigators in basic duty uniform wearing gloves, masks and CSI vests stood around watching as two of their officers confronted a woman in the yard. A CSI tech was standing rather dejectedly nearby, leaning on what appeared to be a metal detector. It was no wonder Caralee had heard voices. The woman was screeching angrily.

It was Jewel Petosky from next door. Caralee sighed, but motioned for Will to follow her.

"Stay close, and don't touch anything," she advised.

The officers seemed to be trying to explain the equipment they were using. Jewel was not letting anyone get a word in edgewise. She seemed startled when Caralee called her name. At first she gave a weak smile at the sight of a familiar face, but then her gaze fell on Will and her smile faded.

Caralee wasn't even sure what the expression she wore could be called. Something about Will's presence certainly had an effect on the woman. She stopped talking and simply stared.

"What's the trouble here, Jewel?" Caralee asked, keeping a friendly tone.

"I…these people want to use these machines," she said, her voice oddly breaking.

"Is the noise bothering you?" Caralee asked.

Jewel shook her head. "No, but I can feel the radiation. That's what they're doing, they're giving me radiation!"

The tech spoke up. "As I told you, ma'am, this is just a metal detector. It's not giving off radiation."

"What right do any of you people have to be here?" Jewel said. "Just go away, stop destroying things. You'll ruin everything. You shouldn't even be here."

"Ma'am, this is a crime scene and we have every legal right to conduct our investigation," one of the officers said with evident frustration. "If you'll please let us continue, we'll be done as quickly as possible."

She was clearly going to ignore him as she'd been ignoring everyone else who would have told her the same thing, but now Will stepped in. Jewel's mouth snapped shut when he spoke to her.

"Please, Mrs. Petosky. I'm your new neighbor, Will Viveners."

Her voice was clipped when she replied. "I know who you are."

"Then you also know that I inherited the house, and I've given these people permission to be here to investigate. They're doing all they can to be quiet and quick. How can I help you feel more comfortable while they're here?"

His words seemed to come so easily and he sounded as if he truly cared about the older woman. Caralee was amazed by the transformation that came over Jewel as her steely gray eyes met Will's generous smile. Jewel must have been surprised, too. She took a wobbly step back from him and seemed at a loss for words.

"Would you feel better if we brought out a chair for you?" Will asked. "You could sit and watch, then you'd know what they're doing."

Caralee wasn't sure having an audience would be such a good thing, but right now anything to calm her and allow them to get back to work was a helpful solution. She watched Jewel closely, wondering what her response would be. She watched Will even more closely, amazed by his gentle attitude toward this stranger who had never shown kindness toward him.

"I used to be able to see the garden from my window, up there," Jewel said, pointing an arthritic finger toward the second story of her home next door. "But now the trees have grown too tall. Everything has gone bad in here... I just want them to go away."

"I understand," Will said. "I want them to go away, too. I'm trying to make the house look nice again and I can't do my work until they finish doing theirs. Why don't we step over here and let them, okay?"

But Jewel just eyed him. She glanced suspiciously over at Caralee, then back to Will. "Why do you want to fix things up here?"

Caralee wondered what the woman hoped his answer would be. Was there a right way for Will to reply? He only took a moment before answering her gently.

"I need the money," he said. "I've got to get the house

ready so I can sell it, and if I can't make that happen soon…well, it'll be too late. You can understand that, right?"

"You're not…going to tear it down?"

Will seemed puzzled by her question. "Um, no, that's not the plan. These people are here to look for clues that might help them understand what happened. You know I discovered a body buried here, right? I believe Chief Paterson talked to you about it."

"Yes, yes. Caralee told me about it and asked me what I knew. But there's nothing for these people to find! They should go away and let you do your work."

"So you don't mind that I'm working on the house?" Will asked.

"No, I'm glad you're working on it. And I saw you helping that little dog, too. That's great."

"I was afraid he might be bothering you, getting into your yard," Will said.

"I don't see him now. Did someone take him?"

"He's staying with me," Will replied. "And he's doing great. I call him Bruno."

For the first time Jewel actually smiled. "That's a good name. I'm happy he's okay."

"Once I get back into this house, maybe I can formally introduce you," Will suggested.

Jewel nodded nervously. "I'd like that."

"I'm sure Bruno would like that, too," Caralee said, sensing the CSI team's frustration as they continued to stand around doing nothing. She nodded to them to continue as she began to lead Jewel back toward the garden gate. "If you want to get to know your new neighbor better, we can step out to the front yard. You might like to chat, tell each other about yourselves."

Jewel seemed to realize she was being removed from the garden. Her smile disappeared again. "What? No, I don't want that. They're turning on their machines again!"

"They're just metal detectors," Caralee repeated. "There's nothing to worry about. See? The investigators walk slowly over the ground and their machines beep if there's metal nearby."

"I know how metal detectors work," Jewel snapped. "I just don't see why anyone needs them. Can't you see? The garden has been dug up already. There's nothing here."

Caralee bit back a reply. Jewel might not see the point in all this, but there could be a gun, or bullet casings, or a knife, or any other metal object that might have been used in a murder and then carelessly hidden here. If they had any hope at all of solving this very cold crime, the team had to be thorough. Aside from weapons, they could also be looking for evidence of other things. If there was one body buried in this secret garden, they needed to make sure there weren't more.

"I took a couple photos of Bruno," Will said, pulling out his phone in a genius effort to distract her. "Come on out to the front yard and I'll show you."

He shot a quick smile toward Caralee and she mouthed "thank you." Jewel was leaning in to see Will's phone and they were, once again, moving toward the exit. The investigators bustled about their work behind them.

They did their jobs too well, as it turned out. Suddenly one of the metal detectors started squealing, indicating something had indeed been found. Jewel whirled around, forgetting all about Bruno and glaring at the workers as they leaned over a spot with a small spade.

"Hey, we found something!" one of them called out.

Caralee wanted to move closer to see, but she hung back with the others. The investigators took their time, carefully documenting their find as they brushed dirt from a small object they extracted from the earth. It was maddening not to be close enough to see what it was.

Finally one of the investigators spoke. "It looks like a necklace."

He held it up. Caralee could see what looked like a gold chain hanging from it.

"I think it's a locket," another investigator said. "And look! There's an engraving on the back. It might be initials?"

At her side, Jewel uttered something under her breath. The woman's expression was unreadable, but Caralee was certain this discovery meant something to her. She gave Will a quick glance, hoping he read the warning in her eyes, asking him to keep Jewel here while she went to look. He nodded.

The investigators were pouring water over the object to get more of the dirt off. One of them was snapping photos. Caralee approached, careful to stay out of their way, but getting close enough for a better look. It was indeed a locket, shaped like a heart. It looked to be made of gold.

"I can almost read the initials," someone declared.

"It's pretty nice," another one said. "Looks like solid gold."

"How long has it been here, can you tell?" Caralee asked.

One of the investigators shook his head. "Not sure, but it wasn't right on top, so it could have been buried for a while."

"Okay, I can read it now," the first investigator said. "I think the initials are *G*…no, *C* and *H*."

Before Caralee could even speculate on those letters, Jewel came rushing over. Will was quick to follow. Caralee stepped toward them, holding Jewel back.

"It was Violet's!" Jewel said loudly. "That was Violet's necklace. She lost it working here one day."

It would have been a logical explanation if Violet's initials had been anything like *C.H.* They weren't.

"Her name was Violet," Caralee pointed out.

"They're her mother's initials," Jewel said. "Her name was Charlotte. It was her locket, then Violet inherited it. That's why she made such a big deal when she lost it, why I remember it."

Now Will spoke at Jewel's side. "Are you certain that was her mother's locket?"

"Yes. Absolutely. No one else's."

Caralee had been willing to accept Jewel's explanation, until now. Jewel spoke with such sharp assurance that she sounded almost angry, as if scolding Will for questioning her. Her confidence didn't ring true. It felt manufactured.

Caralee tried to catch Will's eye, but he was almost intentionally not looking at her.

"I think we should go now," Will said, taking Jewel by the elbow. "Your identification of the necklace will help them a lot, I'm sure."

Jewel pulled her arm away. "Maybe I should hold it, for safekeeping."

"No," Caralee said. "We're going to keep it for a while."

"You won't learn anything from it," Jewel muttered. "It was her mother's."

"Come on," Caralee insisted. "We should leave and let them finish their work."

Jewel tried to protest, but Will took her arm gently again. He looked her square in the eye and spoke very pointedly.

"I'm sure they'll look after your friend's necklace. Are you certain there's nothing else you should tell them about it?"

She blinked, met his eyes evenly, then shook her head. "No, nothing else."

"Then we should go now," Will said.

Obediently, Jewel followed. Caralee was left shaking her head. She had no idea what it was, but she had the distinct feeling those two knew something she did not.

Chapter Thirteen

"I'm glad you're feeling much calmer," Caralee said when they were in front of Will's house. Jewel fidgeted, wringing her hands.

"They're wasting everyone's time in there," she mumbled, glancing over her shoulder.

"Procedures are in place for a reason," Caralee reminded her. "Won't everyone feel much better when we learn what actually happened here?"

"No," Jewel said defiantly. "Some things are better left buried—they should stay forgotten."

Caralee glanced at Will. His surprise at the woman's bitterness was matched by her own. Jewel Petosky obviously knew more about their crime scene than she'd been willing to admit. But just how much did she know, and why was she lying about it?

"Mrs. Petosky, you were their closest neighbor. If you know something, especially if it involves my father, please tell us," Will said.

For a moment it seemed that his pleading tone might have some effect on her. She gazed back at Will, almost as if Caralee had ceased to exist. Then the moment was gone. Jewel shook her head with finality.

"No. I don't know anything. Now leave me alone!"

Angrily, she turned from Will and hurried away. Brokenness was evident in her face; chasing after her would only upset her more. Jewel wasn't about to give them any information right now—she'd made that clear. They'd have to wait until whatever had triggered this outburst could be soothed over. If only Caralee had any idea what it might be.

She and Will stood silently as Jewel ambled up to her front door, then slammed it behind herself. One of the deputies had been watching. He came up to Caralee.

"Do you need me to go over and get her for you?" he asked.

"No, she's distraught right now," Caralee said. "We'll let her calm down. I can check on her later, once the CSIs have finished up. Maybe she'll be willing to talk to me then. For now, let your guys know to just keep an eye on her. Obviously all this is very stressful for her."

The deputy agreed. Caralee sighed and glanced up at Will as they walked back to the driveway at his house. She wondered how stressful this must be for him, too.

"She knows more than she's telling us," Will said softly.

Caralee agreed. "I just wonder what it could be. And did you notice the way she reacted to that locket? It means something to her."

"I saw that. Do you think she'll tell you about it when you go back over there later?"

Caralee shrugged. "Maybe. Or maybe she'll talk to you. What was that rapport you had going on between you? For a few minutes, it seemed like you really got through to her."

Now he shrugged. "Who knows. Maybe it's just because I'm a stranger?"

"Or maybe it's because you're *not*. If she's hiding a secret about your father, something she doesn't want people to know for whatever reason, she might be more likely to confide in you. You are his son, after all. Maybe that means something to her."

"I'd be happy to try talking to her again, if you think it would help. I don't know, though. It seems like maybe just seeing me upsets her. I can't really tell whether she likes me or hates me, to be honest."

"And that's exactly why I think you might be the one to get her to open up. You have an effect on her, Will."

"But is that a good thing, or a bad thing?"

"I guess we need to find out," Caralee said. "But first, are you hungry?"

"What?"

"It's way past lunchtime. Want to go get a sandwich?"

Apparently, she'd said the magic words. He lit up and gave her a grin, his lips quirking at one corner and his eyes sparking with anticipation. The man even had the nerve to run a hand through his tousled hair. She tried not to melt a little bit inside.

"I thought you'd never ask!"

Will dunked another steak-fry into his ketchup and contemplated his next words. They'd managed to keep their focus on small talk for a while, but with their lunches half eaten, he knew it was time to ask about her conversation with his mother. So far she hadn't brought it up.

"So you said you got a hold of my mother today?"

"I did. She was glad I called."

"Glad? I can't imagine that. What did she say?"

"Not a lot. We didn't talk long. I told her who I was, and assured her that you were just fine."

"I'm sure that was a huge relief for her," he said, not bothering to keep the sarcasm out of his voice. "She probably assumed you'd call to say I was in some sort of trouble. Again."

"No, she sounded honestly glad to know you were okay. I told her you'd made a lot of progress on the house, but that finding a body in the backyard was a huge surprise for everyone."

"Did she offer any ideas how it got there?" he asked.

"No. She seemed credibly shocked by it. Mostly, though, she was worried about you, Will. Maybe things aren't perfect between you, but she's still your mother. I hope you'll try calling her again. She didn't have anything to say about the body you found, but clearly she assumes it's your father."

"Does that make her a suspect?"

"I have to look at everyone. But honestly, I believed everything she told me. And I think she'd like to hear from you. For so long, it was just the two of you. You must have been really close then."

"We were," he answered slowly. "For a lot of years."

"Then the stepfather came along?"

"Right. Of course, he was great at first, but you know how that turned out. It was just…a lot for a family to go through."

"I can imagine. How did she even cope? She must have felt horribly alone after your stepdad left and you… well, you know."

"Went to prison. Yeah, I know."

"I'm sorry, Will. I don't mean to keep bringing that up."

"It's okay," he said, and realized for the first time he meant it. "It's a pretty big part of my life. The people who know me, well, they're going to have to know about that."

"And anyone who knows you is going to understand that it isn't who you are," she said. "I made that mistake at first, but I was wrong. You are so much more than your record."

"Thanks, Caralee. That means a lot. I just wish…well, I wish my mother could see it that way."

"She doesn't?"

"What my stepfather did really hurt her, and I was a part of it."

"But you were young! You didn't mean to get involved in his crimes, did you?"

"No, of course not. I argued with him, told him I'd turn him in. But…well, there were other factors."

"What does that mean?"

"It means it wasn't just about me, I had to think of other people. I'm sorry, Caralee. It's not something I want to talk about. Can we please drop the subject?"

"I don't want to pry, Will, but you've got so much to carry on your own. Don't you think maybe it would help if you could open up just a little bit? Share some of the burden with a friend?"

He was surprised by her words. Was that what she thought of him? He was her friend? He knew they worked well together; he'd even felt that maybe she enjoyed his company. But had they somehow become *friends*? He wasn't sure how he felt about that—being friends with a cop.

Then again, she wasn't just a cop. She was someone who recognized that he was more than just his label. She'd shown him respect he hadn't earned. She'd trusted him when he knew most people wouldn't. And she'd made him smile.

Yeah, Caralee was a lot more than just a cop. She really was his friend.

But unlike Will, Caralee had a lot of friends. Right now, one of them called her name. She turned from Will and waved excitedly at a well-dressed, athletic guy with an expensive haircut who had just entered the restaurant. He was smiling just as eagerly and heading straight for her. She jumped up and gave him a big hug.

"Tad! How wonderful! I heard you were coming back to town," she exclaimed. "Are you really staying for a while?"

"A little while. It's great to see you, Caralee. I heard you're pretty busy right now, but I hope you'll find time to get together and catch up."

"Of course!" she promised, then made the obligatory introductions. "Tad, this is Will Viveners. Will, this is D.R.'s son, Tad Fields."

As if she needed to give him the guy's full name. He could have guessed who it was, with his flawless features, charming manners and oozing confidence. He was exactly as Will expected him to be—perfect. Probably not even a parking ticket on his record.

"Ah, my father was just telling me what happened,"

Tad said, reaching out his hand to shake Will's. "It's nice to meet you. Sorry your welcome to Blossom Township had to be so dramatic. A body in the backyard? That's crazy."

"Yeah. Crazy," Will agreed.

Now D.R. appeared, cheerful as ever. If he harbored a grudge for the way Will had questioned him earlier, he gave no indication of it. He greeted them and beamed over his son.

"Yep, my boy is home. The conquering hero! He's been offered VP in his firm, you know. Youngest VP there ever, in fact."

Caralee seemed duly impressed. "Wow, congratulations, Tad. That's really exciting."

As expected, well-mannered Tad appeared humbled by the praise. "Thanks, but it's not a done deal. I told dad they were *considering* offering it to me, but that's all. It's not time to start bragging yet."

"You're taking the financial world by storm, so I'm going to brag," D.R. said. "But come on, they've got our table for us. We'll let these two finish their lunch. They've got an investigation to get back to." Now he turned to Caralee directly. "I guess you've decided to let this guy help you out. That's nice. I'm sure he knows a few things about police procedure."

It was a dig and Will knew it. Caralee probably did, too, but she smiled sweetly and played nice until D.R. pulled his son away. Will didn't miss the little backward glance Tad gave Caralee as he left.

Did anybody get that excited to see an old friend? Will hoped they didn't solve this case too quickly, because as soon as they did, Caralee would have free time on her hands—free time for someone like Tad. Whatever budding friendship she and Will had would end up on the back burner.

"It's great to see him again," she said, her eyes still following him.

"I'm sure. You've known him all your life?"

"Since we were kids," she replied. "I'm happy he's doing so well. To be honest, I thought he'd go into something more creative, but I guess financing can be creative, right?"

"The way my stepfather did it sure was," Will remarked. "You might want to watch out for that."

But she just laughed off his warning. "No, Tad's a good guy. He cares about people. He wouldn't get sucked into anything shady."

"The good guys are the easiest targets," Will said. "Especially if they care about people."

"Sorry, I didn't mean to be insensitive. Want to talk about it?"

He knew he should tell her. She was watching him intently now, waiting for him to speak. She already knew about his convictions, knew about his stepfather and his shaky relationship with the mother he adored. He might as well give her the rest of the story.

"You saw my record," he said. "You know what I was charged with, what I pleaded guilty to."

"Yes, various charges connected to real estate fraud. It must have been pretty hard for you to give testimony about your stepfather's crimes and your involvement with them. But you did it. You told the truth."

"But that's just it, Caralee. I *didn't* tell the truth.

Those things I pleaded guilty to? They weren't my mistakes. I didn't actually do it."

"But you confessed!"

"I lied."

She seemed stunned. "Will...why would you do that?"

"Because it wasn't just about me."

"You lied for your stepfather?"

"No. Not for him. I lied because if I didn't, he would have taken my brother away."

"You have a *brother*? You haven't mentioned him. Why not?"

"You're a cop, Caralee. I know you said we're friends and I should share things with a friend...but you're a cop. There are some things you just can't know about."

She looked like he had just thrown her dinner in her face. She sat up straight in her chair and took a deep breath.

"I see. You're protecting your brother, aren't you? And you think that if I know about it, I'll stick my nose in and make all sorts of trouble. Because I'm a cop, and that's what cops do."

"Caralee, it's not like that. I just don't want to put you in a difficult spot. If I come clean about what happened, you might have no choice but to report it."

"Is your brother a minor? Did something bad happen to him? Because yes, I would definitely have to report that."

"He's seventeen now, but no, it's nothing like that. He did commit a crime, though, and I'm not letting him go down for it. He was just a kid, and he didn't hurt anyone! I already served four years. Nobody else needs to suffer."

"What are you covering up, Will? You might as well tell me. If it helps, I can remind you that crimes committed in Pennsylvania are out of my jurisdiction."

He knew she was mostly joking, trying to put him at ease, and he appreciated the effort. Did he dare tell her his story? For Zach's sake, should he keep a tight hold on his burden, or would it be all right to share it with her?

Finally, he let out a resigned sigh. "My younger brother, Zach, was involved in bribing a public official—someone pretty high up, actually."

"This was four years ago? He would have only been thirteen years old then," Caralee pointed out. "How on earth did he get involved in something like that?"

"My stepfather, of course. Zach is really my stepbrother. He was just a toddler when our parents got married. My mother raised him, she's the only mother he's known. But our father—my stepfather—wanted to get Zach into the family business. He knew he couldn't ask me to do some of what he needed done, so he had Zach do it."

"But he was a child!"

"And he didn't realize what he was getting involved in. My stepfather had him picking up bribe payments and delivering falsified documents, posing as a bike courier. They were doing deals under the table, faking inspections, selling property without a clear title, all sorts of illegal things. Hush money was coming in and going out, keeping everybody quiet."

"And you knew about all of this?"

"Not for a long time. When I finally caught on, it was too late."

"So how did it all fall apart?"

"Zach messed up. One of the packages he delivered was a few hundred dollars short. The crooked inspector who was supposed to get it took offense. He thought he'd make a statement by sending his goons after Zach. They put my brother in the hospital."

"Oh no!"

"Yeah. My mother called the pastor to come pray with us and poor Zach confessed everything to him. What did our loving pastor do? He could have called the cops to go after the goons, but he didn't. My stepfather made a sizable donation that encouraged him to keep quiet. While Zach was lying there, black and blue, no one did anything for justice!"

"So that's why you aren't a big fan of churches and ministers."

"My stepfather sat in that church pew every Sunday with us, pretending to be a fine, upstanding man. In reality, he was a crook who let thugs get away with beating his son. Then he abandoned his family rather than admit to his crimes."

"And you took the blame, to protect your younger brother."

"Our father could have stepped up, could have gotten out of his racket before someone really got hurt. But he wouldn't do that. Instead, he was going deeper into it, dragging Zach and my mother right down with him. I couldn't let that happen, could I? So I made some anonymous tips."

"You turned him in?"

"I gave the cops reasons to start investigating some

of his deals. I thought surely the threat of prison would make my stepfather go straight."

"It didn't?"

"No. He decided to take Zach and my mother on the run. But what kind of life would that be? My mother didn't deserve that, always looking over her shoulder, wondering if today was the day they'd get caught. And Zach had a whole future ahead of him! He wanted to go to high school, play football, plan for college. I couldn't let him be turned into a fugitive."

"I can't believe your stepfather would do that!"

"It didn't take much to talk him out of it, actually. In the end, we made a deal. He agreed to leave on his own, to go away and never contact our family again. I would confess to being involved in the crimes so Zach wouldn't get pulled into the investigation, and that would be that. My stepfather got off scot-free, while Zach and my mother didn't have to live under a cloud."

"And you spent four years in prison for something you didn't do. It hardly seems worth it, Will."

"Of course it was worth it," he said, surprised she didn't understand. "He's my brother. He'll graduate soon, but they're barely getting by. How will he get to college? My stepfather says he'll pay, but only if Zach comes to live with him. *That's* why I have to sell this house. If I don't get some cash soon, Zach might end up working for my stepfather again in some other country!"

Caralee could hardly believe what she was hearing. No wonder Will hadn't wanted to talk about his past. It would be hard enough to talk about things he had done, but it must be very painful to revisit the hurt and betrayal that went along with paying for things he *hadn't* done. She wished more than ever that she hadn't judged him so harshly right from the start.

"I'm so sorry you've had to go through all this," she said. "And how did your mother take it when you made this sacrifice?"

"She believed every word I said. That's part of the problem…why she still hasn't returned my phone call. From her point of view, sadly, I'm the reason her husband left. I'm the criminal in the family."

"What about your brother? Does he understand just how much you've done for him?"

Now she could see real pain in his expression. He shook his head sadly.

"I don't know. I haven't been allowed any contact with him since…well, since it happened. My mother lets me know how he's doing, but she doesn't want me to be a bad influence, I guess. The whole time I was in prison, Zach was about the only thing we did talk about when she'd send an occasional letter or take my phone calls."

"But you should tell her what happened! She needs to understand, Will. You should tell her that—"

"What? That the man she was married to for ten years is the worst kind of person and would rather ruin us than admit to his crimes? That he endangered Zach's life and sent me to prison? No, I can't tell her that. Especially not now when it looks like the first man she loved was a thief and an arsonist…maybe even a murderer."

Caralee realized she was just staring at Will, possibly with her mouth hanging open in disbelief. "You can't possibly think she'd rather believe lies about her own son than know the truth about her husband? She loves you, Will. And she deserves to know, even if it hurts."

There was so much pain in his eyes that she didn't know if her words actually got through to him. After a pause, he took a long breath and shook his head.

"You're right, of course. But how else could I protect her?"

Caralee had to smile at his selfless—but clueless—admission. "You aren't like anyone I've ever met before, Will Viveners. I'll bet your mother is stronger than you think. She raised you, after all."

Before she could be rewarded with another one of Will's signature smiles, Caralee's phone began ringing. She jumped, startled, and quickly pulled it out of her pocket. Her body went cold as she saw the ID on her screen—it was the hospital.

She answered immediately. It was a nurse on her grandfather's floor. She was assured right away that he was in no immediate danger, but they had noted a decline in his overall health. He seemed lethargic, his blood pressure was erratic, and he was refusing food. They just wanted her to know and suggested maybe she ought to visit. He could use some cheering up.

"Your grandfather?" Will asked as she got off the phone.

"Yes, he's having some sort of decline today."

"Is it serious?"

"I don't know. Serious enough that they felt the need to call me. I should probably go over there."

"Of course you should," he agreed, flagging the waitress to get their check. "I'll go with you."

"No, that's not necessary."

"I won't go in and bother the man, but you shouldn't have to go alone. You got me to share all my burdens with you, so now why don't you return the favor and let me share some of yours?"

She liked the way he put that. He hadn't wanted to trust her, yet somehow he did and had allowed himself to open up. Maybe now it was her turn to trust him.

"All right. I'll let you come with me, but only if I can introduce you. I think Grandpa will like you. You're living in his house, after all. He ought to at least meet you."

They paid quickly, left the restaurant and were walking into Grandpa's hospital room ten minutes later. He smiled when he saw her.

She entered first, unable to ignore the pallor of his usually ruddy cheeks. He was slumped back on his pillow, his bed raised so he could sit up. She was glad the nurse had called; he didn't look well at all.

"Hey, Carebear," he said weakly.

"Hi Grandpa. Are you up for some company?"

"Always! Come on in. I see you've brought a friend."

His glance fell on Will, his gaze assessing him head to toe.

"Grandpa, this is your houseguest, Will Viveners."

He gave Will a smile nearly as warm as the one he'd had for Caralee.

"Nice to finally meet you, Will. Caralee says you've been taking real good care of the place."

"I'm trying to, sir. It's a beautiful home and I really appreciate you letting me stay there."

"Well, you couldn't very well stay at your place. So tell me, how is the investigation going? Do we have positive identification yet?"

"No, not yet," Caralee said. "But you shouldn't worry yourself over it. I'll keep you posted as we have any new information, I promise."

Grandpa chuckled, which turned into a coughing spell. Caralee glanced up at Will. She could see he was concerned, too. Even someone who didn't know Grandpa could tell he wasn't well. He certainly hadn't looked this weary and pale yesterday. What had happened to cause this decline?

"I'm sorry," Grandpa said when he caught his breath again. "I don't know what's wrong with me. I was feeling good earlier. I must just be tired. I get so many visitors, you know."

"You're hosting parties when you're supposed to be resting?" Caralee teased. "Who do I need to scold? Who's been wearing you out?"

"Oh, it's not so exciting as all that. Frank and Geneva were here for a while. They brought my church newsletter for me, then D.R. stopped in, probably to see if I was heading for a nursing home and would want to sell my house." He laughed again, but more carefully this time.

"I think you're a long way from a nursing home," Will said. "Caralee tells me she's just keeping your desk warm at work, that you'll be back in no time."

"That's the plan," Grandpa said. "I'm going stir-crazy here. It'll be good to get back to work. So come on, get me up to speed on the case. What did the CSI find there today? Anything good?"

"Not much," she said with a sigh. "The last message I got said they'd found rusty tools, an old container for weed killer, one random shoe, broken pots and bits of trash. One thing did stand out—a gold locket in the ground, not with the body. We were there when they found that. It had some initials on it. You don't, by any chance, know what Violet Viveners's mother's name was, do you?"

Grandpa thought for a moment. "Now let's see… Violet's maiden name was Sanders. Her mother's name was… Charlotte, Charlotte Sanders. Yes, that's right. They lived on a farm just out of town. Violet used to run around with some of the same kids my brother did back in school. Why do you ask?"

"There were initials on the locket, *C.H.* The neighbor, Jewel Petosky, said Violet had inherited it from her mother. But those aren't be her initials."

"Well, it could be a maiden name, of course," Grandpa suggested. "I have no idea what Charlotte's name was before she was a Sanders. That's way before my time."

"We can look it up," Caralee acknowledged. "Other than that, there's nothing new."

He asked a few more questions about the case and she gave him brief answers. There was little to tell, so she shifted into light conversation about his house and how well Will was taking care of it. Of course they laughed over stories about Bruno; Grandpa was especially happy to think of a dog in his home again.

Finally, he nodded and yawned. Caralee knew he needed to rest. His lunch tray sat on the table nearby and he hadn't even touched it. That, especially, made Caralee worry. Grandpa never turned away food.

"Can I get anything for you?" she asked him as his eyes began to droop.

"Actually, I think I'd like to take a rest now. Maybe

you could lower my bed a little? Sorry to put you to work for me…"

"It's no problem at all," Caralee assured him.

Will offered to get more ice for the pitcher beside his bed, and Caralee resituated his pillow and adjusted his blanket. Grandpa yawned again. He seemed to try to speak, but his words were somewhat slurred as he relaxed back into his bed. Caralee took his hand and gave it a squeeze.

He smiled at her. His eyes were sleepy but full of enormous love.

"I'm going to be all right, Carebear," he murmured. "I just need a little nap."

"Of course Grandpa. Would you like me to dim the lights?"

He didn't answer. He was already asleep. She sat at his side, listening to his steady breathing. The heart monitor showed a solid rhythm, which comforted her. He just needed sleep. She couldn't ignore her worry, though. The room around her went blurry as her eyes welled up with tears.

Will returned with the pitcher and positioned it where Grandpa could reach it when he woke. Caralee quickly dabbed at her eyes with a tissue. This was just a temporary setback, not a cause for alarm. Grandpa was going to be all right.

She tossed the tissue into the trash can, smiling when she saw the paper cup with the name of a local coffee shop on it. Someone had thought to bring Grandpa some of his favorite coffee this morning, so that was very nice. He'd obviously drunk it, too. That was a good sign.

"He was much better yesterday," she whispered to Will as they quietly let themselves out of his room.

"I'm sure he's just tired," Will said. "It's cute how he calls you Carebear."

She rolled her eyes but smiled in spite of her embarrassment. "I hate it, but that's what he calls me."

"He obviously loves you very much."

"Yeah. I don't know what I'll do if—"

Her dismal thought was interrupted by the nurse at the station. "I'm glad you could come in. Is he sleeping now?"

"Yes, he's awfully groggy. And…have you noticed that he looks pale today?"

"We've been monitoring him. You're right, and I noticed his speech wasn't as clear as usual. I'm sure it's nothing, but I did inform his doctor. He ordered bloodwork."

"Thanks, I'm really glad you're looking out for him. Do you know if he's eaten anything today? I saw that his lunch hasn't been touched."

The nurse thought for a moment. "I didn't come in until after his breakfast, but I did see one of his visitors brought him a coffee and a cookie. He ate that."

"Thanks. Just let me know if there's anything more I can do for him."

The nurse smiled gently. "I will. Don't worry."

Easy for her to say.

Chapter Fourteen

It was a new day. This morning was half over and Caralee checked her phone—yet again—for messages. She'd fretted for Grandpa all night, but this morning he seemed slightly better when she stopped in to visit. He still didn't have much of an appetite, but his color was a bit better. The doctor promised to have the results of his blood work soon. She headed off to the crime scene and spent the next few hours occupied there.

It was still before lunchtime when an email from the medical examiner arrived. They had results on the body—positive ID and cause of death. Thanks to Will's DNA sample, they determined this really was his father's body. Willard Viveners, Sr. was their victim.

And he was murdered. *Poisoned.* A high concentration of some sort of chemical was found in Willard's body. The examiner listed it as a "pesticide," but the official name was unfamiliar to Caralee. But "pesticide" certainly rang a bell. It was a lead they could follow up on.

Now she just needed to break the news to Will. Unfortunately, he was taking Bruno to the vet this morning. It didn't seem right to just text him the information, so she left a message asking him to call as soon as possible. He needed to hear this from her.

Meanwhile, she would look at the items the CSIs had found in their search. Aside from the bits of trash and garden items, she turned her attention to the weed killer container. She was told that particular product had been off the market for more than twenty-five years, so it could possibly be from the time of the murder. She flagged it for further study.

Work concluded in the garden and Caralee went out to the front yard. The investigation should finish up inside the home today and if all went well, Will could be back in his own home as early as tomorrow. He'd be happy to hear that. It would be nice to have some good news for him along with all the rest of it.

She was just about to phone him again when someone called her name.

"Caralee?"

She turned to find Tad walking toward her. "I thought you might be here today. They've still got the CSIs hard at work, I see."

"Hi Tad! This is probably low-key compared to some of the police activity there in the big city. We're pretty boring around here."

"No, it's never boring—it's home," Tad said. "You guys finding anything? My dad says it's been thirty years, so there probably aren't many clues left. It's like putting a puzzle together, huh? Lots of little pieces. You don't know which ones fit until you really get in there and start working."

"Something like that."

"So I see a sheriff's car on the street, and is that van from the state? I guess it's complicated, working a scene like this."

"We're a small town," she explained. "The house is in the township limits, so it falls under police jurisdiction. The county sent in the CSI team from the sheriff's office and the body has been sent to medical examiners at the state."

He nodded, his brow furrowing as he seemed to be etching her information in his memory. "I see. So who's in charge of the site, then?"

"I am," she said. "I'm coordinating."

"And everyone works pretty well together? Sometimes on TV we see them fighting over who's in charge and all that."

"Well, this is real life. We get along because we're all working for the same goal."

"Solving the crime."

"Finding the truth," she amended. "At this point, we *suspect* there's been a crime, but there's still a lot we need to learn. The important thing to remember is that a person was buried here, and we want to be respectful of that."

"Cool. Right. That's good… Don't forget the human side of it."

To her surprise, he pulled out a notebook and dashed off some scribbles. He was taking notes about her crime scene? She leaned in to see, but he flipped the notebook closed and went back to glancing around.

"How many people are here on-site today? Is the CSI team pretty big?"

"I think there are three from the CSI unit today, plus two deputies on hand. What's with the questions? Is this your new hobby? Not planning to get rid of some rivals back at your big VP job, are you?" She laughed, hoping he would, too.

"It's just interesting," he said, preoccupied watching two team members carry a large black case into the house. "What's that for?"

"I'm not sure," she said. "But come on, catch me up on you, Tad. What brings you home and how long will you be here?"

"I had some vacation time saved up," he said simply. "Thought it would be nice to get away from the city, clear my head for a while."

"You're staying with your parents?"

"No. I've rented one of those Bay View condos."

"Those are nice!"

He gave an easy shrug. "I've got some stuff to think about."

"That big promotion, right? That's really awesome."

"Yeah, thanks. But about this case…did they find anything interesting inside the house? My dad told me there's a rumor about—"

Before he could finish, a vehicle pulled up, taking one of the few empty spots on the street in front of the house. It was Will in his familiar truck.

She waved at him as he climbed out and headed toward them. Tad seemed happy enough to see him, but she wasn't sure Will returned that sentiment. Come to think of it, he hadn't seemed too impressed with Tad when they met yesterday. What was it about him that made Will bristle?

"Good morning," she called. "How was the vet appointment?"

"Bruno was as good as he could be and the doctor says other than some minor skin irritation and being underweight, he's got a clean bill of health."

Caralee was relieved to hear it. She turned to Tad to fill him in. "Bruno is a stray puppy Will took in. Today was his first vet appointment."

"Sounds fun," Tad said. "Congratulations. Is he here? Did you bring him?"

"No, I dropped him off at the place where I'm staying while my house is—as you can see—off-limits." He turned to Caralee. "How's your grandfather today?"

"A little bit better, thanks. But did you get my message?" She lowered her voice and turned her back slightly on Tad. "I wanted you to know we've got the DNA results. Maybe we can go somewhere and—"

But Tad was walking away, moving closer to the house to get a better look at what was going on inside. She had to leave Will and go deflect him.

"Hey, you really should stay out of their way. I know it's cool, but it's still a crime scene. As Will said, it's off-limits."

Suddenly a CSI investigator named Kate came out and made a beeline toward Caralee. "Hey, I just thought I should let you know," she began, an odd look on her face, "we found something…interesting in one of the closets upstairs."

"It must be the safe!" Tad said excitedly.

"What safe?" Caralee asked, turning from Tad to Will. He merely shrugged at her.

"That's what I was about to tell you," Tad said. "My

dad says there's a rumor the old lady kept a safe full of money in there. It's supposed to be hidden behind a secret panel."

Will shook his head, laughing. "News to me! I certainly haven't found a safe full of money."

Kate met Caralee's eyes with a serious expression. "Well…it might not be entirely a rumor."

"You found a safe full of *money*?" Caralee asked.

"We have no idea what's in it," Kate replied. "But it's a few years old, and it was hidden behind a panel. Somebody was hiding something. We'll need a specialist to open it…unless you have the combination somewhere."

Caralee glanced at Will. He shook his head, as perplexed by this discovery as everyone else seemed to be. Everyone besides Tad, that was. He had a smug look on his face.

"Cool!" he said, pulling out his notebook again. "The safe is real."

"When will the specialist be here?" Caralee asked.

Kate shrugged. "I'm not sure. My boss is calling him now. Maybe this afternoon? Maybe tomorrow?"

So they'd have to wait to find out what was inside this secret safe. Surely Tad's rumor couldn't be true? But hey, given there was a body buried in the backyard…one thing was certain about Violet Viveners: there had been a lot more going on with that woman than Caralee had ever guessed.

She met Will's gaze. There were things he needed to know, too. She still had to tell him what the DNA report found. It would be a lot for him to take in.

She watched him, wondering if he was struggling with anxiety, all these things hitting him at once. He was watching her in return, but didn't appear to be anxious. In fact, he gave her one of his grins. If he felt anything, it seemed to convey amused resignation.

"Too bad I didn't pick up any safecracking skills in the joint," he joked. "Who knew that would come in handy now?"

Will watched in amazement, once again awed by the quirks of small-town life. Caralee had been called inside regarding this new safe discovery. Tad was pacing the yard on his phone and Jewel was poking her head out her front door, spying and eavesdropping on everyone. It was hardly surprising at all when an unfamiliar middle-aged couple showed up.

"Hello!" the man called as they walked up the driveway. "We're looking for Caralee Patterson. Do you know if she's here?"

"She's inside," Will said.

"Oh, and I suppose we shouldn't go in there," the woman said.

"No, you shouldn't," Will confirmed.

"Are you with the police?" the man asked.

Will shook his head. "No. I own the place."

Both of them reacted visibly. The man looked like he'd just seen a ghost, and the woman looked like she'd swallowed a bug. Before Will could even process these expressions, they were both smiling again.

"You're Willard Viveners, Jr.!" the woman exclaimed.

"My goodness, what a blast from the past," the man said. "It's a pleasure to meet you."

"You look like your father," the woman said, tsking as she shook her head sadly.

"And you are…?" Will asked.

"Oh, I'm Geneva DeBonet and this is my husband, Frank. He used to be your father's business partner."

So they were the DeBonets! Yes, they certainly fit his mental image of them. In their gardening attire, they didn't look much like murderers, unless the victims were aphids and cutworms.

"I've heard your name," Will admitted. "It's good to finally meet you. I'm sure Caralee will be out here at some point. It's not an emergency, is it?"

"Oh, no, no," Frank said. "We just…well, to be honest, we were hoping the investigation would be done and she might let us peek into the garden."

"As you can see, it's not done."

"Obviously not. That must be very inconvenient for you," Frank said. "I heard you're staying at the police chief's house?"

"I've been looking after things there, cutting his grass, getting the mail. But I'm sure I'll be back here before too long. I'm not worried."

Geneva, however, looked worried. "And then you'll go back to your renovations?"

"That's the plan."

"You're hoping to sell the house, right?" Frank asked. "You're not looking to stay in Blossom Township?"

"It's a nice place, but I plan to sell once I've renovated."

"Pity you have to take so much time for that," Geneva said. "You know, the market is very slow here. You might consider selling it as is, cut your losses."

"Right now I can't exactly do anything with it," Will remarked. He wasn't sure he liked the way Geneva was eyeing his property, and her words certainly didn't fit with what he knew to be true. D.R. wanted to get his hands on this place, and now it seemed the DeBonets did, too. And they didn't even know about the safe in the closet. Or did they?

Tad was finally off his phone and sauntered over. "Oh, hey, Frank and Geneva. It's good to see you!"

They appeared overjoyed to see him. "Tad! How nice that you're home," Geneva said.

"I just told my dad that the rumor about that safe turned out to be true," Tad said loudly. "He's been following this case, took coffee in to see Caralee's grandpa this morning so they could discuss it."

"What's that about a safe?" Frank asked.

"That rumor about the old lady keeping a secret safe in there," Tad said, jabbing his thumb toward the house. "Well, the investigators just found it!"

Frank gasped and Geneva put her hand to her throat.

"Is it…have they opened it?" she asked.

"I don't believe it," Frank uttered.

"They've called in a specialist to crack it," Tad explained.

Frank glared at Will. "Did you know about this?"

"Not until just a few minutes ago when they found it," Will replied. "I'm not sure what to think of it, though."

Another car pulled up at the curb, this time blocking the driveway. A young woman got out. Will recognized her as the assistant at D.R.'s real estate office. She looked around, then smiled broadly when she saw Tad—he seemed popular with everyone in town.

Geneva greeted the young woman. "Hello, Emily. I suppose you're here getting the scoop?"

"I just thought I'd check in, see how the investigation is going," she said offhandedly. "Have they found anything new? Oh, hello. You're the owner here, aren't you?"

Will nodded. "Yes, and you work for D.R. Fields."

So not only did D.R. have his son here scoping out the place, he'd sent his assistant, too.

But Emily shook her head. "I'm not wearing that hat today. I'm also a reporter for the *Blossom Bulletin*."

Will had heard of it. "The local newspaper. So this is a newsworthy event?"

"Of course," Emily said. "I hope Caralee can give me a statement. Our weekly print edition comes out tomorrow and I'd love to have an article ready. I might get front page!"

"Oh, look, here's Caralee now," Geneva said.

Sure enough, Caralee was leaving the house and walking their way. She greeted them but seemed distracted. Or maybe she was just feeling overwhelmed by the masses who were gathered at her crime scene. Tad, the DeBonets, a journalist and even Jewel, who had given up trying to be subtle. She was sitting on her front stoop, glaring at everyone.

"Can you tell us anything yet?" Emily asked. "What do you know about this safe that's been discovered?"

Caralee seemed surprised that Emily would know about it. She glanced at Will, so he tipped his head in Tad's direction. Caralee should know he'd been the one who blabbed.

"Um, I can't say anything about it yet," she announced. "A specialist who can open it will be brought in."

"Can't you just take it out and hit it with something?" Tad asked.

"I'm sure we could," Caralee said, somehow being polite in the face of his ridiculous question. "But there could be evidence inside and we want to preserve that."

"What kind of evidence do you expect to find in it?" Emily asked, holding her phone out to record Caralee's answer.

"We have no idea. It could be empty, for all we know."

"Or it could contain money, or letters, or weapons… and all those things could have fingerprints and even DNA, right?" Emily asked.

Caralee frowned. "We won't know anything until we open it and we are going to do that carefully. Our safe expert can be here tomorrow. I will make a statement at that time."

"But what about the body that was recovered?" Emily went on. "Has there been a positive identification on that yet?"

Caralee shot Will a pained look. He understood what that meant. She *did* have a positive ID; she'd been waiting to tell him in person. That had to mean his DNA sample must have proven a positive match for the deceased. The body he'd found in his backyard really was his long-lost father.

He'd known this was a probability; he didn't know he'd feel so much emotion over it.

"We have run some DNA comparisons…" she said, but her voice trailed off as she watched Will's face intently.

He gave her a nod and pretended he was totally okay with this. She needed to make the announcement. It would have been nice to have a little time to prepare before it was public knowledge, but Caralee's job was serving the public. They had a right to know her efforts were getting results.

"Yes, we have a positive ID," she said finally. "The body we recovered was that of Willard Viveners, Sr., former resident of this home. Based on the condition of the body and items found with it, we estimate he died approximately twenty-nine years ago. As to cause of death, that is still being determined. I'm not in a position to speculate on anything else regarding this case. I'm sorry I don't have more for your newspaper, Emily, but I will keep you informed."

"Thank you, Caralee. That gives us something."

"Now, I'm sorry to be the wet blanket, but I'm going to send everyone away." Caralee smiled, though her words were quite firm. "Our CSIs are completing their investigation inside the house, and the area will remain off-limits until at least tomorrow. It's still an active crime scene and not the local hangout. Okay?"

Before Will could decide whether or not she was dismissing him, too, she called his name.

"Will, we need you to come inside and answer some structural questions. You know the house and can probably give us the best answers."

"Yes, I probably can," he said.

It was a boast, really. Petty, but Will couldn't help himself. He gave Tad a triumphant smile as he turned to follow Caralee toward the house. Tad was left alone; there was nothing for him to do but obey Caralee's orders and leave.

Chapter Fifteen

Will spent the next few hours home with Bruno. Caralee had her hands full with the investigation, and Bruno really needed some exercise out in the backyard. He was coming to love the time they spent chasing a tennis ball out there. The goofy pup still didn't comprehend that he was supposed to bring the ball back to Will, but he sure loved running after it. Will grudgingly did all the retrieving.

It wasn't just Bruno who benefited, though. Will appreciated the distraction. He still wasn't sure how he felt about finally knowing where his father was.

Why had his dad abandoned him? Now he knew: because he was dead. Had most likely been murdered. That, of course, brought on a whole new slew of questions. Who did it? And why?

It would take some time yet to figure those out. For now, Will was getting used to his new reality. He wondered how his mother was coping.

He'd called her again and left a message. That had been several hours ago. Now it was dinnertime and she still had not called him back. Was she ever going to? Was she really that determined to punish him that she wouldn't even respond when he told her his father's body had been positively identified?

It seemed likely. Her pain ran awfully deep; she'd been broken when his stepfather left and Will went to prison. His stepfather must have told her quite the pack of lies before he ran off. Will had no idea what she'd actually been told about him; what really hurt was that she'd believed it.

But he had no control over that. She needed to know the truth about his father, and he had told her. If she had nothing to say to him about it, that was her prerogative. He somehow needed to let go and find peace.

But how to do that? In the past he would have turned to prayer and scriptures. His faith had brought him peace. He might have confided in a friend, too. Where was he supposed to find peace now that he had left all those things behind?

Well, his faith might have been left up high on a shelf somewhere, but he still had at least one friend, didn't he? Caralee. Her faith was near and dear to her, too. Was there any way she might let him borrow her faith for a while? No, it probably didn't work that way.

Besides, she had enough of her own worries. She was coordinating three agencies as they worked on this case, she had journalists and local busybodies to juggle, and a sick grandfather to fret over. His heart really went out to her.

How long had it been since he cared that much for another person? It felt good, actually. He liked learning about her, getting to know her preferences and her sense of humor. He liked worrying over the same things she worried about. He liked watching the clock, wondering when he'd get to see her again.

Yeah, it had been a long time since he'd felt this way. In fact…he only just now realized exactly how strongly he felt. In such a short time, he'd come to truly care about Caralee. She mattered deeply to him, and maybe he even hoped for something more than friendship.

He certainly hadn't intended to develop these feelings—that didn't fit with his plans at all. He was very sure it didn't fit with Caralee's, either. But the more he thought of her, the more tender he felt toward her. A longing that had been dormant for so many years was waking up from a long, lonely slumber. There was a huge hole in his life—and it was exactly the right size for a blue-eyed, red-haired cop.

His cell phone rang in his pocket, making him jump. He tossed the ball one more time for Bruno, wiped his hands on his jeans and answered. It was Caralee.

"Oh, good, I'm glad I caught you," she said. "Are you busy right now?"

"No! Not at all. I'm glad you caught me, too." He probably sounded embarrassingly eager. "What can I do for you?"

"Um… I'm at the hospital."

"Oh no! Your grandfather? Is he okay?"

"Well, he had another decline today, a bad one. The doctor did some more tests and…well, he's stable and sleeping now but…it doesn't look good."

"I'm so sorry, Caralee. Can I come over there? Would it help if you had some company?"

His breath caught in his chest when she sighed, sounding relieved—happy even—that he'd asked.

"That would be great. Are you sure it's no trouble? I just don't want to leave him, but I really wish my family was around."

A million emotions welled up in Will. He understood how she felt, being alone when the world was crashing down around you. No one should have to feel that, especially not Caralee. He'd move mountains if it meant seeing her smile again, hearing her voice filled with hope and confidence once more.

"Give me ten minutes," he said. "No, eight minutes. I'll be there."

Caralee felt a little silly, calling Will as she had. Surely she had other friends she could call, her pastor, even. But Will had been her first instinct, for whatever reason. He didn't need to come rushing to her, though. She was an adult.

But she really needed someone to talk to, someone to keep her from wallowing in worry and self-pity. Honestly, she wanted that person to be Will.

She'd been sitting at Grandpa's bedside for the past hour. He'd slept fitfully, restless and pained. When one of the nurses mentioned flowers had arrived and were at the reception desk, Caralee was grateful for the excuse to get up and move around. She'd gone to collect the flowers, but then instead of heading back up to the room, she wandered into the hospital chapel. It seemed the place to be.

"I thought I might find you here," Will said behind her.

She turned and smiled as he entered the room. He'd

made it a lot faster than she expected. Just knowing he was with her, it felt like even the air was a bit lighter.

"Did you have to hunt for me?" she asked.

"No, for some reason I came here first. From the way you sounded on the phone… I don't know, the chapel just seemed like the place you would be."

He'd been right, obviously. The chapel here at Blossom Memorial Hospital was a peaceful space, with walls that were a soft, warm mauve, and narrow windows of stained glass. A beautiful painting of praying hands hung on the front wall. Someone had placed fresh flowers on the small altar there. Gentle instrumental music played in the background.

She was glad Will had thought to come here first. Grandpa need to be lifted up now, and so did she. Will's caring reaction and comforting presence were definitely a blessing.

"How's he doing?" Will asked, sliding into the chair beside her.

"He's resting. We're not sure what sent him into such a decline again. He became lethargic, feverish, and his blood pressure dropped pretty significantly."

"Does the doctor have any guesses?"

"The blood work yesterday showed he'd become anemic. We're not sure how or why. His last tests a week ago showed he was fine. Today his iron count is dangerously low. It could be…well, the cancer could have spread somewhere they don't know about."

"That's concerning. I'm really sorry, Caralee."

"Me, too. He was doing so well! After just a few more treatments, we were expecting to hear that he was into remission. Now I'm afraid of what we might find."

"I get that. But you know fear isn't what he'd want you to feel."

"I know, and the Bible tells us over and over to fear not and I'm trying, but it's hard when I just can't see things getting better."

"I don't think 'fear not' is a commandment," Will said. "I'm pretty sure those words are meant to give comfort. Scary things happen and of course we're afraid. But fear is *not* the destination, it's the thing we simply walk through. And we don't have to walk alone."

She narrowed her eyes and studied him. "Now you're a theologian. I thought you'd given up all this faith business?"

"I don't know what my faith is anymore," he said. "But I do know that you still believe. And maybe that helps me believe a little bit more."

"Then maybe we can believe together? Would you pray with me, Will?"

She didn't want to put him on the spot, but she hadn't been able to reach Pastor Donaldson and the hospital chaplain was off today. If Will was willing to encourage her faith, maybe he could pray with her, too.

"Of course I will," he said.

"I think God's listening even if we don't talk to him on a regular basis," she said, then smiled.

He smiled in return and reached for her hand. She easily gave it. He squeezed it and bowed his head with her.

She led the prayer, asking for guidance and praying for healing and physical well-being for her grandfather, but also for wisdom for the doctors and hospital staff. And she thanked God for good friends. Will gave her hand another squeeze as she came to the end of the prayer. She added some silent sentiments before finishing.

"In Jesus's name we pray this and ask you to continue Your work in our hearts, whatever that is. Amen."

For a moment they sat in silence together, heads still bowed. He continued holding her hand. Such a peace seemed to flow over them that she didn't want to interrupt the moment. It was truly an answer to prayer; her fear seemed to have gone and she felt secure where she was.

A slight knock from the doorway broke the stillness. She pulled her hand back from Will and turned. Grandpa's doctor stood in the doorway holding his tablet. She couldn't read his expression. Or didn't want to.

"Sorry to interrupt," he said softly. "But we have more results in from the blood work."

She glanced at Will for assurance. For the doctor to come find her here, it must be important, and probably wasn't good. What a blessing that she'd been given these moments of peace to prepare for it.

"Come in, Doctor," she said. "What have you found?"

He came toward them and pursed his lips, then glanced toward Will. "I'm sorry, but perhaps Miss Patterson would prefer privacy?"

"It's okay," Caralee said. "He's a family friend."

But the doctor didn't seem convinced. "I'm sure, but…this could turn out to be a police matter."

That was the last thing she expected him to say. "A police matter? Well, by all means, fill me in."

He nodded and then proceeded to explain. "As you know, we ran more blood work for your grandfather. I expanded the panel this time and came up with something…unusual. I'm not sure how it got there, but we found an alarming level of boric acid in your grandfather's system. A toxic level."

"Boric acid? Isn't that some kind of cleaner?" she asked, trying to make sense of his words.

"No, not quite. It's from the same element, but boric acid is a refined form. It has medical and industrial applications, but it can be pretty dangerous."

"What's it doing to him? Can we neutralize it?"

"It's caustic, so we're looking at the possibility of tissue damage internally. It all depends on how it was introduced into his system, and in what quantity."

"Is it in any of his medication? Maybe he accidentally took too many pills."

The doctor shook his head. "No, it's not an ingredient in anything he's taking. If he were at home, I might suggest that he'd accidentally exposed himself—it's a common pesticide. He could have touched it, or even possibly ingested it."

"But he's been here. His blood work was just fine last week and he's been feeling so well, up until yesterday. He hasn't gone anywhere or done anything. He's eaten his meals from the hospital cafeteria. How could he possibly have gotten into this stuff?"

The doctor was very careful with his next words. "That's why I'm worried this could be a police matter. We haven't had any other patients display symptoms, so it doesn't appear to be environmental contamination or tainted cafeteria food. At this point, I can only speculate that he was given something that was brought in from the outside."

"I brought him cookies a few days ago," Caralee said. "But since then I've been busy with this investigation. I haven't had time to bring him anything extra. Where could he have gotten it?"

"He had a coffee brought in yesterday. Didn't the nurse mention that?" Will asked.

Caralee remembered the coffee cup in the trash can. "Yes! One of his friends brought him a coffee, and a cookie from that little place he likes."

"Who was it?" Will asked.

She wished she knew. "The nurse simply said one of his friends."

"It's okay. We'll figure this out," Will assured her.

"I'm afraid I saw another one of those coffee cups in his room again today," the doctor said. "He was feeling much better this morning, so we thought it was good that he was up for company and getting treats."

"Then he got sick again," Caralee said. "Someone put something in that coffee! Who visited him this morning?"

"The nurses on his floor might remember, or you could check down at reception," the doctor said. "Visitors have to sign in there."

"I'll do that," she said. "And you're certain there's no natural way he could have ended up with this in his system?"

"No. I hate to say it, but someone has intentionally been poisoning your grandfather."

Caralee's heart clenched at the thought. Who would do such a thing? Everyone loved Grandpa. He'd been in the hospital over two weeks and there'd been no sign of poisoning until just now. Why would it suddenly begin?

Could it have anything to do with the case? Did someone think Grandpa knew something about it and was hoping to shut him up?

What if they had already succeeded?

"Doctor, you said you worried about internal damage from this poison. Do we know how bad that could be?"

"That's the other thing we need to talk about," the doctor replied. "Boric acid poisoning can be very serious. Damage may still be occurring as long as it's in his system. We need to get it out, and the usual treatments aren't effective, I'm sorry to say."

"Well, what is? Surely there's something you can do for him," Will said.

The doctor nodded. "Dialysis is generally considered the best option. We need to clean his blood."

"Is that dangerous?" Caralee asked.

"That's the good news." Finally the doctor's expression brightened. "Other than taking some time, it's relatively risk-free. As long as…"

"What?"

"As long as there isn't already too much damage. We'll monitor his condition. I'm hopeful that after the dialysis, we'll see his levels return to normal. I promise, though, we'll do whatever he needs to get through this, Caralee. And for now, no visitors."

"Thank you, Doctor." She tried not to let the heaviness of this new information weigh her down. "I'll do whatever I can to find out who's behind it."

Will gave her a reassuring smile. She was glad he was here with her. She returned his smile and would have told him how much she appreciated him, but her radio interrupted. It was Vicki in dispatch.

"Sorry to bother you, Chief, but be advised I've just dispatched a unit to that murder scene. There's a break-in. We got an anonymous call."

"All right. I'm heading over there. Thanks."

She had to go. The bouquet for Grandpa still sat next to her and she wondered what to do with it. The doctor generously offered to carry it up to Grandpa's room for her, since he was going that way.

"Thanks. I picked up the flowers at the reception desk, then came in here to pray. I thought I'd be going back up."

"They're very lovely," the doctor said. "So many good people really care about your grandfather."

Caralee glanced at the card attached to the flowers. She hadn't thought to check it before; she'd been too preoccupied. The card, however, did not fill her with hope or appreciation for good friends. She stared at it, then handed the card over to Will.

"Look at that! What do you see?"

He glanced at the card, then raised wide eyes to meet hers. "It's the same writing as that letter I got!"

The same person who had written that threatening letter had written this get-well wish for Grandpa. The signature was right there, with a bold flourish.

Geneva DeBonet.

Caralee did not hand the flowers to the doctor. "Sorry, Doctor, but this bouquet is going with me. The CSI team might want to run a few tests on it. You said the poison could have been ingested or even just touched?"

"Yes, it could have, although if it came into contact with skin we would have seen redness or burning."

"All the same, I'm taking the flowers. Carefully."

She thanked the doctor for all he was doing. If anyone could help, it was Dr. Girard. He was the best. Will followed as they left the sanctity of the chapel.

"We have to stop by the reception desk on our way out," she told him. "I still want to find out who brought that coffee to Grandpa this morning."

"No need," Will said to her surprise. "I just remembered who visited. Tad mentioned his father went to see him today. He took him coffee."

Chapter Sixteen

"Someone must be trying to get the safe," Caralee said as they rode in her car over to Will's house in response to the report of a break-in.

"Makes sense," he agreed. "All of our suspects knew about it, that you would be opening it tomorrow and expect to find some kind of evidence inside."

"We should have known someone would try this."

"Well, at least we can catch them in the act," Will pointed out. "Who do you suppose we'll find?"

"D.R. seems to be the prime suspect right now. He poisoned my grandfather, probably to keep him quiet. And we know Tad told him we found that safe."

"That would certainly fit. He's been hounding me to sell the house quick—he's wanted it all along, probably for the safe."

"But why on earth did Geneva write that horrible letter to you?" Caralee asked. "Where's the connection?"

"To scare me away. Maybe they're in it with D.R? Frank and Geneva showed up today hoping you'd let them into the garden. Clearly they were looking for something, too."

"But what?"

"I don't know, but they heard about the safe, so if someone is breaking in to find it, I wouldn't be surprised if it's one of them. And to be honest…when I heard the doctor say boric acid, I thought about Frank."

He wasn't sure if it was fair to accuse the man, but at this point all possibilities needed to be considered.

"Why Frank?" she asked.

"Because of what he does," Will explained. "He had that pest control business. Boric acid is a common ingredient used for that sort of thing."

"And he'd have easy access to it."

"Absolutely. When I worked for my stepfather's company we used it in some of our properties. Someone like Frank would know all about it."

"So maybe it wasn't in the coffee. Maybe Frank put it in with flowers from Geneva. Not this bunch, but the ones they sent him a couple days ago."

"This doesn't narrow down the suspects much. We've still got everyone except Jewel."

At that very moment they pulled up in front of Will's house to see Jewel Petosky herself standing in the front yard, shaking her finger at one of Caralee's officers and yelling a blue streak. Will recognized the young officer from that first day when he'd discovered the body. The young man looked completely confused about what to do. Caralee uttered a weary sigh.

"Maybe Jewel isn't off the suspect list after all," Will said, only partly joking.

"I'd tell you to wait here, but you might as well come

along," Caralee said. "You did a good job helping to settle her down before."

"But he's in there now!" Jewel was saying as they approached. "You've got to go in!"

"I'm sorry, ma'am, but this is a crime scene. Please go back to your own house."

"He'll ruin everything, he's in there now!" Jewel insisted.

The officer seemed very relieved to see Caralee. "She's insisting that someone is inside the house," he explained.

"Thank you, DeKalb. You're sure no one is inside?"

"I've been here all afternoon," the officer replied. "Since Sergeant Billings is stuck on desk work, I'm covering his shift."

Will shot Caralee a quick glance. "You've got Billings on desk work?"

"Until he completes some additional de-escalation training, yes," she replied quickly, then turned back to DeKalb. "And no one has come or gone?"

"No one. I've been sitting out front the whole time."

"He didn't come in the front," Jewel screeched. "That's what I'm trying to tell you! I saw him go over the wall."

"Ma'am, that wall is eight feet high," DeKalb said. "It's unlikely that—"

But Will interrupted him. "Wait, do you smell that?"

Everyone paused a moment, then Caralee cried out. "Smoke! I smell smoke—from the house."

Immediately Will started for his house. Caralee was at his side, calling over her radio. Jewel pushed past Officer DeKalb, ready to charge in with them. Will kicked in his own front door and smoke billowed out. For one moment all he could think of was the fact that at least Caralee was safely outside with him, but then she shoved him aside and ran in.

He dove into the murky smoke after her.

"No, go back, Will," she ordered. "If someone's in here, I'll find them."

There was a loud noise from the kitchen at the back of the house. Someone coughed, and it sounded like they tripped over something. Caralee was pushing Will back, clearly planning to go deeper into the house on her own. Will fully intended to follow but he was suddenly bumped from behind.

Jewel squeezed past him, nudging him out of the way as she hurried through the hazy room toward the stairway. Will called her, alerting Caralee to her presence.

"Jewel! Don't go up there!" Caralee shouted.

But Jewel ignored them and began climbing the stairs. What on earth was she thinking? If someone was setting fire to the house, running upstairs would be the worst thing to do!

"I'll get her," Will said. "You and DeKalb find out who's in the kitchen."

The smoke was getting thicker. Will could barely see Caralee even though he was just a few feet from her. DeKalb had joined them, so after a brief moment of hesitation, Caralee moved forward, calling the officer to follow. They had a very limited window here. If they couldn't drag the culprit out of this house in seconds, it could become too late.

Will bolted up the stairs, two at a time. He caught Jewel on the landing, hanging onto the knob at the top of the banister post. She seemed to be clinging to it for dear life.

"Come on, Jewel. We've got to get out of here," he said, taking her by the shoulders.

But she fought him. "No! It's still in here. I've got to get it."

His eyes burned and he rubbed them, realizing that Jewel wasn't just hanging on to that knob, but she was pulling at it, twisting as if she wanted to remove it.

"What are you doing?" he asked.

"Help me! We've got to get in there."

"In where?"

"Inside the post!" Jewel said, tugging even harder. Her words were raspy as she choked on the rising smoke.

Will reached for her hands, prepared to pry her loose. The knob was turning, though. As he helped her with it, the whole top of the post came off. He knew the stairway was going to need some work, but he didn't expect it to come apart so easily. What was Jewel after?

"Grab it, get it out of there," she ordered him.

The heavy square post at this corner of the stair landing was apparently hollow. Will reached inside and found something lodged in there. He felt around, barely able to grasp the top of a cylindrical object.

"Is it there? Can you get it?" Jewel asked, practically vibrating with excitement.

He gripped it tightly with the tips of his fingers, sliding it slowly upward. It seemed to be a tube of some sort. It was nearly the same size as the post, so it was wedged pretty good. He worked it back and forth, inching it upward until at last he slid the whole thing out: a fat mailing tube, sealed at both ends.

Jewel ripped it from him and clutched it to herself.

"Come on," he ordered. "You've got your treasure, now I'm getting you out of here."

There was no hope of seeing their way down the steps, so Will had to go by feel. Thankfully, Jewel co-operated and allowed him to lead her. At the other end of the house he could hear noises, but by now he and Jewel were both coughing so hard he couldn't tell what they were.

Was the place ready to come crashing down? Had Caralee found the perpetrator? Would she be able to get out in time? Will forced himself to concentrate on leading Jewel through the smoke and toward the bright area that he hoped was the front door.

They made it out onto the porch and nearly ran into a deputy running up the front steps.

"Here, help her," Will said, handing Jewel off. "I'll go get the others!"

"No, stay out here," the deputy said. "The fire department is on their way."

"Caralee is still in there!" Will called before staggering back in.

He hid his face in the crook of his elbow, hoping to block as much of the cloying smoke as he could. His feet stumbled over things on the floor—lumber, tools, power cords. None of it mattered. He had to find Caralee.

He felt his way to the kitchen. He could see the flames now, feel the heat. He tried to call out, but all he could do was choke. Footsteps staggered toward him.

Officer DeKalb came from the kitchen, dragging someone. Tears and smoke blurred Will's vision, but he could make out the form of a man. DeKalb pulled him along.

"She's in there, get her," DeKalb sputtered.

Will nodded and charged past him into the kitchen. The fire seemed to be at the back wall where the cabinets and kitchen sink were, blocking passage to the back door. He could smell something chemical, too. *Accelerant.* This fire was no accident!

"Caralee," he growled into the smoke. How was he going to find her? What if she had fallen or was unconscious?

Gingerly, he crouched and began feeling the floor. The air was only slightly easier to breathe down here. The visibility was just as bad.

"Ouch!" he choked as someone stepped on his hand.

Suddenly someone was tripping over him, tumbling down on top of him, elbows or knees knocking him in the head. He lurched to one side, toppled onto the floor. Caralee was there, tangled with him, scrambling to recover her footing.

"What are you doing?" she rasped.

He struggled to catch his breath, drawing in a lungful of smoke. He began choking.

But Caralee was already helping him up. She got a handful of his shirt, roughly pulling him from the room. He hit his shoulder on the doorjamb as they went through, back into the front part of the house. He was relieved to catch a glimpse of her uniform beside him, directing him toward the front door.

Soon they were on the porch, gasping and choking. He wished he could get a good look at her to reassure himself that she was fine, but his eyes were a stinging mess. Somehow they made it down the steps and into the front yard without falling flat on their faces.

"Did DeKalb get out? Jewel?" she gasped when they could finally breathe again.

"Yeah," Will answered as best he could. "Jewel is fine, and there's DeKalb."

He pointed to the officer, looming over the figure he'd hauled from the kitchen. Who was it? Will rubbed the soot from his eyes.

"It's Frank," Caralee said, obviously anticipating his next question.

"Frank DeBonet? He started the fire?"

"I don't think he expected so much smoke quite so quickly," Caralee said, her own voice strangled and raspy. "When he's able, we'll get some answers."

There was another crashing sound inside the house— the cabinets had probably come down. Will's future was going up in smoke, literally right before his eyes. For half a moment he was tempted to rush back inside and do whatever he could to stop it.

But Caralee grabbed his arm. "No, Will. It's too dangerous—please don't go in there."

Her swollen eyes were filled with genuine concern. He could only smile in response. Of course he wouldn't do anything that might give her more reason to worry, or to endanger herself by rushing in after him. He could see it in her face; if he went back into that billowing smoke, she'd be right there at his heels. He could never allow that.

"I'm not going anywhere," he assured her. "We're both staying right here."

Sirens sounded nearby, drawing closer. The fire department would be here soon. At this point, Will could only pray they would save the structure. And if they couldn't, he would still utter a prayer of thanksgiving for everyone getting out safely.

Caralee returned his smile, until she was distracted by a deputy.

"Chief, you'd better come look at this!"

The deputy was standing over Jewel. She sat on the ground, clearly struggling to breathe. The mailing tube she'd rescued was still clutched in her grasp. Caralee shook her head, looking concerned.

"Thanks for getting her out of there, Will," she said. "The paramedics will take a look at her."

"You'd better look at that tube," Will informed her. "She ran inside to get whatever it is."

Caralee knelt down beside Jewel and spoke quietly, asking to see the tube. At first Jewel was hesitant, then her watering eyes glanced up and it was as if she saw Will for the first time. Slowly she broke into a smile.

"This is for him," she said, finally relinquishing her prize.

Caralee accepted it but gave Will a questioning look. He could only shrug—he'd never seen it before today and had no idea what it could contain. Carefully, Caralee opened it.

"That's all for you, Will," Jewel said as stacks of money came tumbling out.

"So Willard did steal the money!" Caralee exclaimed.

Frank must have been paying attention from several yards away. He groaned loudly. "He really had it! He actually had the money."

"Of course he had the money," Jewel snapped. "I

gave it to him. But I told him he'd best never trust *you* with any of it."

"So this is the money everyone thought had burned in that fire?" Caralee asked, flipping through the cash. "*You* gave it to him?"

"I did. I gave it to him for the baby. For him!" Jewel pointed directly at Will.

"You knew about me?" he asked.

"Of course. I'm your auntie."

Caralee did her best to control the chaos that broke out. The fire department had arrived, along with several other deputies, the sheriff himself and the other three police officers who were on duty. Neighbors were gathering on the sidewalks, gawking at the activity and speculating on what it all meant.

Further conversation with Jewel was hindered by an oxygen mask the paramedics strapped over her face. Caralee's heart ached for Will as he stood helplessly watching the firefighters drag hoses and equipment into his house. The smoke was even thicker now as water vapor was added to the mix. Caralee wished she could focus on Will and offer him reassurance, but she had Frank to deal with. He was being arrested for arson and resisting arrest, among other things.

To add to the tumult, Geneva showed up, frantically searching for Frank and demanding that someone explain to her what was going on. Caralee hoped Will understood she'd be forever grateful when he stepped in and got Geneva's attention. She stopped arguing long enough to listen.

Caralee filled in the sheriff on what had been going

on and was happy to see that Jewel still seemed feisty and just as nosy as ever. She hadn't suffered from significant smoke inhalation, and Caralee hoped Will had fared just as well.

When she was certain everything was under control, she motioned for Will to allow Geneva to come speak with Frank. DeKalb had cuffed him and let the paramedics load him onto a gurney. He'd be sent to the hospital for evaluation before being brought to the station for booking. Geneva deserved to know what he'd done. Will deserved some answers, too.

"Oh, Frank, what were you thinking?" Geneva cried when she came to him.

Caralee nodded to the paramedic and stepped in to make sure Frank didn't try anything silly. Will remained at Geneva's side. Frank eyed him nervously.

"Sorry…it wasn't anything personal," he began, sighing in defeat. "I just couldn't let them get into that safe tomorrow."

"Did you think the money was in there?" Will asked.

"Of course not," Frank said, shaking his head. "I never dreamed he had any money!"

Geneva furrowed her brow at him. "But you told the insurance people that half the money that burned was Willard's."

"Yes, of course I told them that, but there was never any money in the desk. I made it up, Geneva. Sorry, but it was all lies."

"But the money I gave you from my family," she questioned. "You said it burned in the fire."

Frank hung his head. "I had debts to pay…debts to people I shouldn't have done business with. Sorry, Geneva, but we were flat broke. When Willard told me he was leaving town and wanted to collect his share of our bank accounts, I didn't know what to do! I never told him I lost all our capital."

Caralee felt sorry for the man. The crushing shame in his voice was tragic. Still, he'd tried to burn Will's house down and nearly killed them in the process. She was surprised Will sounded so compassionate when he stooped down to meet Frank's dejected gaze.

"So you burned your own business and made up that story about money in the drawer," Will said.

"Yeah," Frank admitted. "It seemed the only thing to do—burn it down and get the insurance payment. I made up that bit about the missing money so Willard would have to go along with the scam. It almost worked, too, and thankfully no one got hurt."

Geneva didn't appear to be as understanding. She was simmering, in fact, her voice becoming shrill. "No one was *hurt*? But we ended up bankrupt! That investigation dragged your reputation through the mud!"

"Only until Willard disappeared," Frank said. "Don't you see? As soon as he disappeared, D.R. figured that meant he'd done it all, so I was off the hook."

"But we were ruined by then!" Geneva said. "I had to quit the garden club! It took us five years to get reinstated."

"I know, and I'm sorry about that," Frank said, shaking his head.

"So you killed my father to put the blame for your crimes on him," Will said, his voice still calm although Caralee noticed him clenching his fists at his sides.

Frank blinked in confusion. "What? No! Oh, no, I

didn't kill him! I thought he'd run off. It's what he was planning, after all. He'd had divorce papers drawn up and he was leaving Violet for good."

"All this time, you didn't know he was dead?" Caralee asked.

"I was as surprised as everyone else when his body turned up," Frank said. "And that money Jewel found is a surprise, too. I sure wouldn't have been trying to burn the place down if I thought it was in there."

"So why were you trying to burn it down, then?" Will asked.

"To keep you guys from finding the safe!" Frank said, as if it were obvious to everyone. "I broke in here a few days ago, but there were too many cops patrolling around. I had to sneak out the back before I got upstairs to the safe. I knew about it because I helped Willard install it years ago."

"And what's in it that you don't want us to see?" Caralee asked.

Now Frank hung his head sheepishly. "The registration for the daylily."

Geneva glared at him. "You mean…registration for *my* daylily? What would that be doing in Violet's safe?"

Frank sighed before continuing. "Because it isn't your daylily, my love. I found it here… I knew Violet had been hinting at registering a new daylily. When I saw it after she died…well, I knew that must be the one. I dug it up and put it in with your seedlings so you could find it and think you'd propagated it yourself. I just… I didn't want you to find out what I'd done. You love that lily so much!"

Caralee waited to intervene when Geneva exploded

with anger, but to everyone's surprise she did not. For a moment she glared at Frank, her face devoid of expression. Then she threw her arms around him and began weeping.

"Oh, you dear, dear man! That is the sweetest thing anyone has ever done for me!"

Caralee could have thought of a few things far more romantic—and legal—that he could have done for his wife, but it was good to see that Geneva still cared for him. She gently pulled her aside.

"We've got a few more questions for you," Caralee said. "For starters, Geneva, you need to tell me about a certain letter that was delivered to Will's house a couple days ago. What do you know about that?"

Now it was Geneva's turn to look sheepish. "Oh, you figured that out, did you?"

"I noticed your handwriting on the card to my grandfather. Why were you threatening Will?"

"Because he'd been talking to D.R." Geneva sneered when she spoke of him. "And I know D.R. wanted to handle the listing for his house and he'd set the price far too high for us. I hoped that if Will was afraid someone was out to get him, maybe he'd be willing to sell quickly and cheap. To us."

"What do you need with another house?" Will asked her.

"Oh, it's not for us," Geneva insisted. "It's for the new nonprofit organization our garden club is starting. We plan to open an education center with a show garden, a place where we can share our knowledge and skills with others, where people can learn to love growing things as much as we do. Obviously, what place would be better for that than Violet's beautiful secret garden?"

"Well, why didn't you just come talk to me about it?" Will said. "I love that idea!"

"I guess we were afraid you'd only be interested in the money, and our budget isn't very big."

"I'd certainly rather sell it to you for a good cause than for you to just burn it down!" He shook his head and gave Caralee a puzzled look. "Are all the people in this town nuts?"

Caralee could merely sigh. "All right, Geneva, I believe you. But if you and Frank didn't kill Willard, who did?"

Both DeBonets shook their heads and shrugged. Frank coughed. From a few yards away, Caralee heard Jewel calling to them.

"I can answer that question!" she announced, pushing away her oxygen mask and swatting at the paramedic who tried to calm her. "I was there when he died. I know what happened."

Chapter Seventeen

"Jewel, you need to let them help you," Caralee said, walking over to the older woman. "They're taking you to the hospital and then we—"

"I don't need the hospital! And where is my money? What did you do with it?"

"I locked it in my cruiser for safekeeping," Caralee said. "And I'm looking forward to your explanation... after the doctors make sure you're okay."

"I told you I'm fine. Where's that boy...where's my nephew?"

"You mean Will?" She glanced up to see him making his way over to them.

Frank was in good hands with the paramedics and she'd already assigned DeKalb to accompany him to the hospital. It was just as well that Geneva was with them. She wasn't causing trouble and she was out of Caralee's hair.

"How are you, Jewel?" Will asked her. "You breathed in a lot of smoke back there."

"I'm fine now," Jewel insisted. "And I'd better tell

you the truth. I should have said something when you got here, Will, but I wasn't sure how much you knew, or if you'd even want to talk to me."

"Why wouldn't I?" Will asked. "You were the one pulling the drapes shut every time I glanced your way."

"I know… I'm sorry. It's my guilty conscience, I guess."

"What are you guilty of, Jewel?"

"Oh, not murder." She chuckled, then coughed, but slapped the paramedic who tried to offer the oxygen mask again. "I'm guilty of other stuff, though. And ashamed of myself. The way I treated your poor mother, Will… I'm truly sorry for that."

"You knew my mother?" Will asked.

"Of course I did! She's my sister's girl, my favorite niece. That's why I'm your auntie! Technically your great-aunt, whether you like it or not."

Will was clearly stunned by this. "I had no idea."

"Yeah, that figures. You probably don't know much about your family, do you? No, we weren't very nice to you. And I was especially rude about it. Oh, I called your mother all sorts of terrible names."

"But why?"

"Because Violet was my dearest friend! And it was my fault… I'm the one who introduced your mother to Willard. I never dreamed they'd end up having an affair! She was so much younger, just finishing college when she spent that summer here with me."

"My mother lived with you?"

"She did! She had an internship at the hospital here and I let her stay with me. Willard came over to spray for bugs—he had that pest control business, you know.

Well, I knew he and Violet were talking about splitting up, but I never dreamed he had his eye on my niece. When she went back to Cleveland to finish her schooling, he started finding excuses to go and visit her. I didn't think anything would come of it, but then…"

"Then I came of it," Will finished for her.

"And Willard got his divorce. I don't think anyone ever knew it, though. He died the same day he got Violet to sign those papers."

"So…he *was* going to marry my mother," Will said.

"Of course!" Jewel said quickly. "That's why I gave him that money. That house was his, but I knew Violet was going to fight him for it. He'd need something to help him with his new family. Plus, I felt guilty for the way I treated your mother. When we found out she was running around with a married man, the whole family turned on her. I heard my sister wouldn't have anything to do with her, or you. I gave Willard the money and told him to be sure to hide it from Violet—she knew Willard had a new family but didn't realize it was with my niece."

"You gave him money so he could leave? It had nothing to do with the insurance scam?" Caralee asked.

"Oh, he hated that scam. Frank had him over a barrel, though, so he kept quiet."

"But…how did he die?" Will asked after a pause.

"It was the day he finally talked Violet into signing those papers. She was spitting mad about it and came over to my house to vent."

"You're sure she didn't kill him?" Caralee asked. "She had the motive."

"I'm positive!" Jewel insisted. "Violet and I were

sitting in my kitchen, drinking tea. My window was open and we could hear Willard next door arguing with someone in the backyard."

"Who?"

"I couldn't tell…it was a man, though. At some point the arguing stopped and Violet went upstairs to the restroom. Next thing I know, she's calling for me to come look. I ran up and from the window saw Willard in the garden, having a tantrum and pulling up some of her favorite flowers. He was drinking the pitcher of hibiscus tea that Violet had made for herself, too. She said he didn't even like hibiscus tea! Well, Violet was furious and I was afraid of what she might do to him, so I followed her over there. By the time we got there, though, he was lying on the ground…dead!"

"Dead?"

"Oh, yes, he was very dead. We figured he must have had a heart attack."

"But you didn't call an ambulance?"

"Violet wouldn't let me. She realized that since she'd signed those divorce papers, she wasn't his wife anymore. That meant she wasn't his *widow*. She wouldn't get the house now that he died! It was all in his name, and he had an heir now. She was my best friend and she begged me to help! So I did. She'd had a fresh bed dug for some shrubs she was putting in. It wasn't much trouble at all to drag Willard over there and just…bury him. It looked really nice after we planted over him, much better than any plot in the cemetery would have looked."

"You didn't think my mother would want to know what happened to him?" Will asked, incredulous.

"I'm sorry." Jewel sighed. "Everything I did was so

very wrong. But I told myself sending that money on to your mother would make up for it. I knew where Willard hid it in that post, I just had to get into the house and get it. But then…"

"Then?"

"Violet took Willard's jacket off the back of a chair where he'd left it," Jewel said. "She found something in the pocket. It was that necklace, the one you found here with your metal detectors. That's when she learned the whole truth."

"You said that was Violet's mother's necklace," Caralee noted.

She knew just by the way Will and Jewel exchanged glances that she'd been misled.

"So those initials really were hers," Will said, shaking his head sadly.

"That's right," Jewel said. "It wasn't Violet's locket. The initials *C.H.* were for Christina Harris—your mother. She'd given the locket to Willard, but I guess he'd hidden it in his pocket so Violet didn't find out. Well, Violet recognized it. For the first time, she realized who Willard was leaving her for, and she blamed me. She was so angry! How could I have known and not told her, my very best friend? She threw the locket into the garden and said I'd betrayed her. After that, she never invited me over again, so I wasn't able to get in and retrieve that tube full of money. I would have sent it to your mother, Will. That was my plan!"

"But I met you here," Caralee pointed out. "When I came visiting here. You must have made up with Violet over the years."

"Well, I was keeping her secret, wasn't I? I made

it a point to come around anytime she had guests—I knew she'd have to play nice in front of others. Oh, it drove her crazy! That's why she hardly ever let anyone come over."

"So all this time you knew my father was dead?" Will said. "And you never once tried to reach out and—"

Jewel was spared the lecture she clearly deserved, when another car pulled up, ignoring the police officer directing traffic away from this street. Before the car had even come to a stop, the passenger door opened and someone jumped out.

Caralee felt the hint of a headache starting as one more player in this confusing drama showed up. It was D.R. and he was not being quiet.

Tad was driving the car. He put it in Park and leaped out, running after his father. D.R. tried to shove him away.

"Why did you bring me here? I told you I needed a ride to the airport!"

"Dad, you can't go to the airport. You can't just run away from this," Tad said, grabbing him roughly by the shoulders and pushing him forward to face Caralee. "Tell her. Tell her what you know."

D.R. merely grumbled angrily.

"Then I'll tell her," Tad announced loudly. "I found a file in his desk with notes from nearly thirty years ago. My dad claimed Willard stole from Frank to pull off an insurance scam, but he knew that wasn't true. He knew Frank set that fire! Go ahead, Dad, be honest for once in your life. Tell them what you knew."

By now all eyes were on D.R. Tad still had a good grip on his shoulders, forcing him to stand up and face his accusers. There was nothing D.R. could do but speak.

"Fine. It's true. I knew Frank set that fire, and I knew he lied about the money being burned. Okay?"

"No, go on," Tad prodded. "You knew the money didn't burn, because you knew it was never there. Frank was broke, but Willard had some cash—it was his, and he never claimed that it burned. It's all there in your notes, Dad. The notes you didn't turn in to your bosses because you decided to shake him down instead."

"Do you know what they were paying me back then?" D.R. said angrily. "I was saving them millions every year, and they gave me grocery store gift certificates for a bonus. It just seemed fair that I should squeeze a little bit out of Willard as the price of my silence—he'd pay me, or I'd say he committed fraud. I had no idea he'd get so irate when I confronted him about it."

A sudden realization hit Caralee. "You're the one who was arguing with him in the garden!" she exclaimed.

D.R. didn't deny it. "Yeah, that was the last time I saw him. I knew he had the cash on him, but he refused to give it up. I told him fine, I would tell my boss that he was trying to scam them."

"And he fought with you, so you killed him!" Will said.

"No, he was alive after the argument," Jewel pointed out. "He died of natural causes."

"But that's just it," Caralee said. "He didn't. Willard Viveners was poisoned. The crime lab found some kind of pesticide in his tissue. They believe it brought on respiratory distress and heart failure."

Jewel and D.R. both appeared honestly surprised. Apparently Frank had been listening in as the paramedics were loading him into the ambulance nearby. He cackled with laughter.

"I knew it! One of you two did him in!" he said. Geneva scolded him to keep quiet, but he just brushed her off. "I don't need to keep quiet, I've already confessed to my crimes. I didn't kill him."

"You had access to pesticides, though," D.R. pointed out. "If anyone had motive to kill him, you certainly did!"

"But I didn't do it!" Frank shot back. "Anyone could have used that poison. You were the one arguing with him just before he died."

D.R. snarled. "He was just fine when I left, sitting in his lounge chair laughing at me while he chugged down that iced tea."

"Chugged it?" Caralee asked. "He didn't even like that kind of tea, according to Jewel."

"According to *him*, it was his favorite kind," D.R. said. "His wife made it especially for him. I remember thinking he must be pretty smooth if he can cheat on her, get a divorce and still have her make his favorite drink."

"Well, someone killed him," Will pointed out, glaring at D.R. "Who else would have access to that pesticide? What kind was it?"

Caralee pulled the information up on her phone. "Something called…paraquat dichloride?"

Frank seemed genuinely surprised. "What? That stuff is serious business! It's not for pests, it's a weed killer and it was banned for a while. Now it's only used for commercial agricultural purposes. I certainly don't keep any of it on hand—not then, not now."

"And I don't use anything like that," D.R. grumbled.

"But Dad…you use pesticides and weed killer all the time," Tad pointed out, eyeing his father suspiciously. "For the properties you manage. Just last week you ordered a bunch of that stuff…what was it, boric acid?"

"I was an insurance inspector back then," D.R. said sharply. "And how do you know about my business anyway?"

"Emily told me."

"Emily? Who's Emily?"

"Your assistant, Dad." Tad frowned as he spoke, and his voice sounded way beyond frustrated. "She works hard for you and you don't even know her name! She told me she was worried you were spending way too much for things and it might be cheaper to hire out."

"Why is she poking into my business? Why does she even care what I spend for supplies?"

"Because she cares about our family, Dad. That's what I've been trying to tell you! Emily and I…well, I came home a few days early and we went to the courthouse. We're married, Dad! I'm quitting my job in the city and we're settling down here, in Blossom Township. Emily wants to be an investigative journalist and I want to do art, so we're creating a graphic crime novel together! Caralee gave me some awesome tips about crime scenes and stuff."

No one seemed to know what to say. Caralee certainly didn't! This was every bit as surprising as a confession of murder would have been. It explained some of Tad's inquisitive behavior, too. But could he have picked a worse time to drop this bomb on his father?

"That is the most ridiculous thing I've ever heard!" D.R. roared.

"I knew you wouldn't understand," Tad snapped.

Caralee took a few steps closer to D.R., determined to keep the focus on her investigation. "Well, I want to understand why you ordered a whole case of boric acid."

"Some of the places I manage have bugs. I use it for that." D.R. hardly sounded confident in his reply.

"What about my grandfather's coffee? Did you use it in that, too?"

D.R. got a wild look about him, then slowly deflated. Shaking his head, he gave a deep sigh. His shoulders sagged.

"I'm sorry. That was a huge mistake—I should never have done that."

"But you did it twice!" Caralee said. "Thankfully I got word a little while ago that dialysis worked and he's going to be okay, but why would you want to kill my poor grandfather?"

"I didn't want to kill him!" D.R. said. "I was careful not to use too much. I just… I was worried he'd remember that my investigation showed no evidence of there being any money—then I started claiming it was stolen by Willard. Once the body turned up, he'd know I lied. I figured he'd jump to conclusions and accuse me of the murder."

"So you thought you'd poison him?" Caralee said.

"I just wanted to distract him, let the case get cold again! I forgot all about those old notes Tad found. I should have burned them."

Caralee just shook her head. "You were our friend, D.R. How could you think poisoning my grandfather would keep us from finding the truth? If you weren't planning to kill him, you must have figured he'd get better eventually and then tell us."

"I thought you'd find the real killer by then! And I'd be off the hook."

Tad looked absolutely disgusted with his father. "So that's why you were running away. That's pretty low, even for you, Dad."

"That still doesn't answer who killed my father," Will said.

Caralee thought about it for a moment, then turned to Will. "I think I know the answer to that."

She was going to share her theory, but another car suddenly showed up, swerving to avoid the police cruiser blocking the road. This time when the car came to a halt, a woman emerged. Caralee didn't recognize her, but she began marching their way.

"Now, who can this possibly be?" Caralee mumbled under her breath.

"Um, it's my mother," Will muttered.

Chapter Eighteen

"What happened, Will?" his mother asked as she joined the crowd gathered in his front yard. "Are you all right?"

"It's okay," he replied. "Everyone's fine."

He supposed with everything that had gone on today, her arrival should not be surprising. But it was. He'd left word for her that his father's body had been positively identified and he'd been dead this whole time. She needed to know this. He'd never expected her to show up in Blossom Township, though.

And the last thing he wanted was a confrontation in front of everyone.

Caralee seemed to assess the situation and quickly took charge. Calling over her radio, she instructed her officers to direct traffic as the two ambulances on site prepared to head out. Deputies asked gawkers to step back, return to their homes. Caralee herself took D.R. into custody and had an officer lead him to a cruiser. Will was especially pleased when she cheerfully congratulated Tad on his marriage; she seemed happy for him.

The plume of black smoke that had billowed from Will's house was quickly becoming clouds of white vapor. The firefighters had worked swiftly to get things under control. Will stepped out of the way as another hose was reeled past him, and two firefighters shouted instructions for each other. So far, it appeared hopeful the house would be saved.

"I'm glad you're not hurt," his mother said, her voice betraying nervousness. "We headed out as soon as we got your message. I wanted to be here with you."

"We?"

Will had a momentary flash of panic that his step-father was with her. That was not the case, though. She waved at the car and to Will's surprise, his stepbrother climbed out from the passenger seat.

"Zach and I, of course."

Zach gave a feeble grin and waved hesitantly at Will. He'd grown much taller since Will had last seen him. He almost looked like a man now. Will didn't bother to hide his joy; he gave a hearty wave, though he would have much rather gone over and hugged him. Which Zach would have probably hated.

"Wow, he's so grown up," Will said.

"He'll be eighteen next month," his mother replied, although Will didn't need to be told. He might not have seen his brother, but he certainly hadn't forgotten him.

"I can't believe you guys are here," he said, then tried to cover his awkwardness with a joke. "Sorry the place is such a mess."

"I'm just glad it's still standing," his mother replied. "Are they able to save it?"

"I think so," he said. "We managed to catch the guy setting the fire, so the crews got here right away."

"Is that him in the handcuffs?" She pointed toward D.R. as he was being helped into the back of a squad car.

"No, that's the guy who was trying to blackmail my father."

"He was? Did he...did he kill him?"

"No, I don't think so. He poisoned the chief of police, though."

"Oh my! You've had a lot going on here."

He had to laugh at that grand understatement. "You have no idea."

Before he could fill her in, Zach trotted up to them. Will could hardly keep from throwing his arms around him, but he remained cool.

"Hey, brother. Good to see you."

Zach looked awkward and uncomfortable, but he smiled in return. "Yeah. You, too. Um, is this your house?"

"Not much to brag about, huh? I was making good progress, though...before this."

"It's not too bad," Zach said, then joked, "Looks kind of...hot."

Will laughed and the tension between them faded away. He quickly filled them in as best he could. Frank and Geneva left for the hospital, and Tad's wife showed up to write another article and offer him comfort as his father was being hauled off to jail. Jewel snapped angrily at the paramedics who continued to fuss over her.

Will's mother watched her and chuckled. "That's Aunt Jewel, all right. She likes to do things her way."

"Should we go over and talk to her?" Will asked.

"Oh, she doesn't want to talk to me. She's made that clear over the years."

"I know, and she told me how much she regrets that," he informed her. "If you're up for an apology, she'd probably like to offer one."

His mother looked doubtful, but Jewel had seen them by now. She was staring at them, as if trying to convince herself what she was seeing was real. She put her hands to her face as Will began leading his mother toward her.

"Christina," Jewel said, her voice cracking as emotion overtook her. "If you've come here to give me a big slap on the face, I can't say I blame you."

But Will's mother could only shake her head with equal emotion. "Auntie Jewel, I'm not going to hit you. What happened to you?"

"Oh, I tried to be a hero," Jewel said with a shake of her head. "Not sure I succeeded. Caralee took the money and locked it up! I guess it's evidence, or something."

Will's mother gave him a puzzled look. "Money?"

"It's a very long story," he said. "And maybe we should find some quiet place to talk."

Jewel cleared her throat and spoke up hopefully. "You can come over to my house!"

Caralee appeared suddenly at Will's side. She must have heard at least part of the conversation. She patted Jewel's arm as she sat on the back bumper of the ambulance she had refused to be loaded into.

"I think that's a wonderful idea," Caralee said. "If you're sure you won't let them take you to the hospital."

"I keep telling these kids I'm just fine!" Jewel insisted. "I've got things to sort out with my family. That's most important right now."

Caralee turned her gaze up to Will. She must have some idea of all the emotions that swirled inside him, the questions and concerns, the anxious hope he was almost afraid to acknowledge. Her smile told him she understood.

"Are you up for that?" she asked him.

He deferred to his mother and younger brother. "If you guys are. We all have a lot to catch up on."

His mother nodded. Zach gave a noncommittal shrug but made no argument. Will took a deep breath and reminded himself to stay calm. He did, however, have one request.

"Will you join us?" he asked Caralee. "There are a couple people I'd like you to meet."

Caralee smiled at his family, then at him. "All right. They can get by without me here for a little while."

Jewel had to sign a few papers for the paramedics, and Caralee issued some orders for her people, but before long they were helping Jewel to her front door. Will wasn't quite sure how much of her shaky movements were caused by exhaustion from what she'd just been through versus sheer nerves. He knew his own nerves were unsteady. He'd gone from being alone in the world to suddenly having his whole family here, plus one friend.

A really good friend, he was happy to say.

"Mother, this is Blossom Township Acting Police Chief Caralee Patterson," he announced. "Caralee, this is my mother, Christina, and my brother, Zach."

Caralee shook their hands. He was happy to note that his mother seemed genuinely pleased to meet her and impressed by the title.

"It's wonderful to meet you in person," Caralee said. "And Zach, too! Will has told me great things about both of you. You're a senior in high school, Zach? And you play football?"

"I will be this fall," Zach said. "It's my third year on the varsity team."

Jewel ushered them into her home. Will hung back to let the others go in first. His mother was commenting on how everything looked exactly the same as she remembered it. Zach seemed mildly interested, and Will felt jittery and unsure what to expect. Caralee touched his arm as she passed in the doorway.

"It's going to be okay," she whispered.

He nodded and thanked her, glad she was here with him. There was no one he'd rather be sharing uncomfortable family moments with than Caralee.

He followed the group into Jewel's living room. It was a place out of time. The decor seemed to have been carefully placed here thirty-five years ago when Jewel moved in. The colors and furniture styles were right out of the decade before Will was even born.

"I never thought I'd be back here," his mother murmured.

"I was afraid you never would," Jewel said. "But I can only blame myself for that. You were so kind to me after my husband died, taking that internship here in town so you could stay with me. And then I treated you terribly. Can you ever forgive me?"

The touching reunion between the two women was heartfelt. Will smiled at his brother, eager to reconnect with him. They'd be getting to know each other all over again. For now, he was happy to stand by and let his mother and Jewel catch up.

Until his full attention was captured by a collection of family photos that hung on Jewel's wall in neat frames. What made Will's jaw drop in amazement was his own face at various ages—framed and hanging with honor among photos of strangers with vaguely familiar features.

"You have *my* photos on your wall!" he blurted out.

Jewel came to his side. "I do. I may have cut your mother out of my life, but she never abandoned me. Every year for Christmas I'd get a card from her with photos of you. I was too ashamed to ever respond, but you've been part of my family all along, Will."

"I had no idea," he said, unable to tear his eyes away.

"I should have told you that first day you showed up," Jewel said. "I've been a stubborn, frightened old biddy and it's about time I own up to it."

With a bit of gentle prodding, Jewel sat beside her niece on the well-preserved couch to explain what had happened all those years ago. Will had relayed the most basic elements of the story in his message for his mother, but of course she had many questions for Jewel. Zach listened intently; he'd grown up with the stories of how his mother's relatives had turned their backs on her, how she'd struggled alone until finally meeting his father and becoming a family. This unexpected reunion was an emotional roller coaster for all of them.

"How are you doing?" Caralee said quietly beside Will.

"I'm wondering just what you said to my mother on the phone yesterday."

"I may have mentioned something to her about you

not actually being a criminal." She pointed to the photos. "So…you're going to need to learn who all those people are. You've finally got a family, Will."

"If they want me," he replied simply.

She chuckled at that. "Well, who wouldn't? You're awesome."

"Thanks. You are, too, Caralee. I hope you know that."

"I like hearing it from you."

She met his gaze and smiled. He took her hand and squeezed it. There was still so much to figure out. So much of his future was murky and unknown, but in this moment now, he knew it would be far brighter than his past.

His mother's elevated voice drew his attention. "All this time you thought it was natural causes, but now they're saying he was poisoned?"

Jewel nodded, then looked over to Caralee for help. Clearly she'd given his mother all the information she had. Anything further would have to come from Caralee. After all, she'd said she thought she knew who had done it.

"Wait…wait," his mother said, clearly holding back her emotions. "We've all been through so much and searched for these answers for so long. I'm just not sure what to do with them now. Can we pray together?"

Caralee was still holding Will's hand and looked at him. "Are you up for that?"

"I think it's a wonderful idea," he said.

A beautiful peace fell on the room. Caralee let it wash over her as Will led them in prayer. She could feel love and strength flowing through him as he asked God for wisdom, compassion and grace as they navigated this new reality they all found themselves in. He prayed for those who'd caused harm and those who'd been hurt.

"And finally, I pray that Zach has the best senior year ever. In Jesus's name, Amen," Will finished.

Zach smiled. Christina and Jewel both had tears in their eyes. Caralee wondered if they knew how far Will had come on his spiritual journey in just a short time. She offered her own silent prayer of thanks that Will had begun to let go of his bitterness and allow himself to seek God once again.

"Thank you, Will," Caralee said. "That means a lot."

"So tell us what you know," Jewel insisted. "If Frank didn't kill him to hide his insurance fraud, and if D.R didn't kill him to get the money, who did?"

"It had to be Violet," Caralee said simply. "She made that tea, didn't she? But why would she have told you he didn't like that kind of tea when D.R. saw him 'chugging' it? She obviously wanted you to think she had made that tea for herself so you'd never suspect she'd doctored it."

"But Violet was with me…we were together when we found him." Jewel's face puckered as she tried to comprehend this.

"She used you, Jewel. You were her alibi. And then she pulled you into her crime by convincing you to cover it up."

"I thought I was just helping her!"

"You were, but much more than you thought. It wasn't only her claim on the house you were protecting. She was avoiding a murder charge, too."

"I had no idea!" Jewel cried. "But won't someone need proof of it all?"

"We've got the proof. Our investigators dug it up—a container of the very poison used to kill Willard was there, and it we know it was from around that time. That particular poison was banned shortly after he disappeared. It's circumstantial, but Violet definitely had motive *and* means. The only trouble is the investigators are going to wonder why you were trying to keep them from finding it."

"I was trying to keep them from finding that locket!" Jewel said. "I was afraid they'd trace it back to Christina and then suspect her. I couldn't have that."

"My locket? You mean the one I gave Willard? I gave it to him so he'd have a piece of me with him as he worked out his divorce. He wasn't looking forward to dealing with Violet. He knew she'd give him some trouble but we never dreamed she might…"

"I know, it's hard to believe," Caralee said. "But there's no other conclusion."

"So it was Violet all along…" Jewel shook her head, slowly digesting what this meant. "I thought she was my best friend."

Christina put her arms around Jewel to comfort her. It was such a beautiful example of love and forgiveness.

Caralee nudged Will. "I think they're going to be all right," she whispered.

Will nodded and reached for Caralee's hand. Did she realize just how deeply he'd come to care about her? It seemed like a very good sign when she smiled up at him and laced her fingers with his.

"I'm not really sure who the prodigal is in this story,"

he said softly. "But it feels like everyone has finally come home. I know I have."

"I think you're right where you're supposed to be," she replied, tipping her face up toward his. "I hope you fall in love with Blossom Township and want to stay here forever."

"I'm not going anywhere," he promised. "I've fallen in love, all right. With you, Caralee."

"Is that your confession?" she questioned, her eyes bright with emotion. "Then I have to admit I'm guilty, too. I love you, Will. I really do."

It was as if everyone around them, all that they'd just been through, simply faded away. He could feel the love flowing between them. For the first time in years, he had reason to dream. Love had set him truly free. The others in the room were all focused on one of the photos Jewel was pointing out to them, so Will couldn't resist teasing Caralee just a bit before leaning to kiss her.

"That's a serious offense, Chief. What do you advise?"

"Permanent custody, I'm afraid."

"Oh, good," he replied. "I was hoping for a lifetime sentence."

Epilogue

"Welcome home!" Caralee jumped as a chorus of voices shouted when they stepped through the front door.

She and Will still had suitcases and bags in their hands, returning from their two-week honeymoon. Her surprise turned to laughter when she noticed the huge banner someone had hung over the mantel on the broad fireplace in her living room. It seemed her whole family was there along with all their friends.

"All right, who let you guys in here?" Will asked loudly. "And why aren't you out there helping us carry in our stuff?"

Bruno bounced into the room, barking and licking both of them. Zach came running from the kitchen, apologizing for losing track of him. He and the young dog had been fast friends from the first day they met. Bruno's fears had faded away and he was a happy, healthy dog now.

The past year had flown by, full of awkward meetups with family members and sorting through legal matters. Caralee's parents had returned from their mission and had been happy to welcome Will into their town and their family. It was clear early on that whatever had been growing between Will and Caralee was the sort of thing to last a lifetime. They'd been engaged before Thanksgiving.

Caralee's investigation wrapped up and the courts dealt with bringing justice where it was possible. D.R. was sentenced for his crimes, so Tad and Emily took over his business and were now thriving with a much friendlier, trustworthy real estate firm while creating their graphic novel on the side. Once Caralee realized Will's animosity toward Tad was based in needless jealousy, she'd had a good laugh and convinced him she and Tad had never been more than just friends. They still were, in fact, but now as couples. He and Emily were with the crowd in their living room, posting photos to embarrass them on social media.

"I'm glad you're back, Carebear," Grandpa said, stepping around the suitcases and the excited dog to give Caralee a big hug. "And just in time to take me to the North Shore Flower Show next week like you promised."

"I know, Grandpa. I remember our date."

How could she forget? He had still been in the hospital recovering when she told him all about the daylily that Violet had named after her, but that Frank had stolen and let Geneva think she'd grown it. When Geneva announced she'd wait a year before introducing it—with the proper name—at the annual flower show, Grandpa had made Caralee pledge to take him so he could admire the bloom that would soon be officially named after her. She couldn't be happier that he was healthy now and ready to go.

"The new house is looking great!" Will's mother called to them.

She was standing beside the wall that Will had designated his favorite place in their new home: the photo gallery. There, beside the fireplace, a large section of wall was covered with framed photos of everyone they loved. When they'd left, that wall was still bare. His mother—probably with help from Caralee's mother—must have taken hours to gather the photos and hang them all so neatly. Right in the center was a candid shot of Will and Caralee at their wedding, hand in hand with giant smiles as they walked out of church on that most special day.

"Now I really *am* home," Will said. "Thanks, Mom. I love it."

They'd bought this house shortly after Will had sold the other. There were far too many unhappy memories there for him even to consider keeping it once it was clear he'd never be leaving Blossom Township. Thankfully, the firefighters had managed to save the house from any structural damage and the Garden Club was happy to get their hands on it. They bought it from Will, then hired him to oversee the renovations.

Frank DeBonet cooperated with law enforcement and stood trial for his actions. He would be spending a few more months in jail, but Geneva was eager to welcome him home. Since his attempted insurance fraud had not actually worked, there were no penalties for that, and the statute of limitations for his original arson had long since run out. Will had been able to forgive him for the recent arson, but they probably wouldn't be inviting Frank to any barbecues in the near future.

The money Jewel had saved from the burning house was initially held as evidence, but eventually returned to Will. He'd asked Caralee if they could use it to put Zach through college and help his mother move closer to them. Of course she'd agreed that was the perfect use for it. With the money from the sale of his house, they'd been able to buy this one. It was another fixer-upper and Will had moved right in. He'd been living here for ten months, working on this house as well as the first house for the Garden Club, and working for Tad and Emily as they contracted him for some of their properties.

Thankfully, Caralee's job had not kept her nearly as busy as his had. Grandpa had come back to the force as chief, and she'd gratefully relinquished his office. The murder case had been closed and life had returned mostly back to normal in Blossom Township.

When her phone buzzed in her pocket, Caralee glanced at it from habit. Seeing a notice from work, she stepped out of the room. It was from the Township Council, on official letterhead, and she tucked herself in the little alcove next to their coat closet to read it.

It was the official announcement: Grandpa would be retiring in six months. She knew he'd been planning that, and of course she was happy for him, but she still hated to see him leave his post. What really surprised her, though, was the rest of the letter.

The Township Council planned to promote her to Chief of Police. Of course she should have seen that coming, but the thought of permanently taking on that role still filled her with concern. Was she really ready for this promotion?

Maybe Grandpa should delay his retirement, or recommend someone else to the Township Council. They'd listen to him. She shoved her phone back in her pocket and turned to march off to confront him.

Instead, she ran smack into Will. She jumped in surprise and nearly tripped over Bruno. Will caught her in his arms and held her steady.

"I like when we meet up this way," he said with a grin. "Why'd you disappear?"

"I got a message…from the Township Council," she said, happy to lean on him. "They want me to take over as chief when Grandpa retires."

"That's awesome!"

"Is it really? What if I'm not ready?"

Will's gaze was intense as he met her eyes. "Of course you're ready, Caralee. You were ready last year when you single-handedly solved a thirty-year-old murder case, you were ready to take on a work-in-progress like me, and you were ready to build a future together. From what I can see, you are ready for anything. You amaze me, Caralee, and I love you."

She slipped her arms around him and held him tight. "I love you, too, Will. I'm glad we're finally home."

* * * * *

Get 3 FREE REWARDS!

We'll send you 2 FREE Books plus a FREE Mystery Gift.

FREE
Value Over
$20

Both the **Harlequin® Special Edition** and **Harlequin® Heartwarming™** series feature compelling novels filled with stories of love and strength where the bonds of friendship, family and community unite.

YES! Please send me 2 FREE novels from the Harlequin Special Edition or Harlequin Heartwarming series and my FREE Gift (gift is worth about $10 retail). After receiving them, if I don't wish to receive any more books, I can return the shipping statement marked "cancel." If I don't cancel, I will receive 6 brand-new Harlequin Special Edition books every month and be billed just $5.49 each in the U.S. or $6.24 each in Canada, a savings of at least 12% off the cover price, or 4 brand-new Harlequin Heartwarming Larger-Print books every month and be billed just $6.24 each in the U.S. or $6.74 each in Canada, a savings of at least 19% off the cover price. It's quite a bargain! Shipping and handling is just 50¢ per book in the U.S. and $1.25 per book in Canada.* I understand that accepting the 2 free books and gift places me under no obligation to buy anything. I can always return a shipment and cancel at any time by calling the number below. The free books and gift are mine to keep no matter what I decide.

Choose one: ☐ **Harlequin Special Edition**
(235/335 BPA GRMK)

☐ **Harlequin Heartwarming Larger-Print**
(161/361 BPA GRMK)

☐ **Or Try Both!**
(235/335 & 161/361 BPA GRPZ)

Name (please print)

Address   Apt. #

City   State/Province   Zip/Postal Code

Email: Please check this box ☐ if you would like to receive newsletters and promotional emails from Harlequin Enterprises ULC and its affiliates. You can unsubscribe anytime.

Mail to the **Harlequin Reader Service:**
IN U.S.A.: P.O. Box 1341, Buffalo, NY 14240-8531
IN CANADA: P.O. Box 603, Fort Erie, Ontario L2A 5X3

Want to try 2 free books from another series! Call 1-800-873-8635 or visit www.ReaderService.com.

HSEHW23

Get 3 FREE REWARDS!

We'll send you 2 FREE Books plus a FREE Mystery Gift.

FREE Value Over **$20**

Both the **Mystery Library** and **Essential Suspense** series feature compelling novels filled with gripping mysteries, edge-of-your-seat thrillers and heart-stopping romantic suspense stories.